"If you
peop...
now's the time," he muttered.

"Are you sure?"

"No, but do it anyway."

Sometimes it simply suited a woman to do as she was told.

The touch of a tongue, the remembrance of a taste once savored and never forgotten. One stunningly erotic kiss to fill the need inside her. One steamy open-mouthed caress to make all those years of loneliness fade away. She wanted that from him.

She took it.

Jake thought he could control this. Here on the pavement in front of strangers Jake figured he could curtail his response to the woman who'd once held his heart. But he hadn't counted on Jianne's absolute surrender to the moment. The way she fed the passion that flared between them. Savored it. Savored him. With lips and with tongue and a single-mindedness that left no room for holding back. The deeper he fell, the hungrier he got, and the more she gave—until finally he broke the kiss and rested his forehead against hers, his heart thundering and his senses reeling from her taste.

He closed his eyes and kept them closed. Kept one of his senses firmly closed to her as he struggled to regain his mind and some small measure of control. "Put your helmet on," he whispered. "We're leaving."

Accidentally educated in the sciences, **KELLY HUNTER** has always had a weakness for fairy tales, fantasy worlds and losing herself in a good book. Husband...yes. Children...two boys. Cooking and cleaning... sigh. Sports...no, not really, in spite of the best efforts of her family. Gardening...yes, roses of course. Kelly was born in Australia and has traveled extensively. Although she enjoys living and working in different parts of the world, she still calls Australia home.

Visit Kelly online at www.kellyhunter.net.

Kelly was a RITA® Award finalist in the Best Cotemporary Series Romance category in both 2008 and 2010, for her novels *Sleeping Partner* and *Revealed: A Prince and a Pregnancy.*

HER SINGAPORE FLING

KELLY HUNTER

~ THE EX FACTOR ~

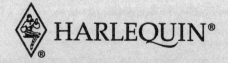

HARLEQUIN®

TORONTO • NEW YORK • LONDON
AMSTERDAM • PARIS • SYDNEY • HAMBURG
STOCKHOLM • ATHENS • TOKYO • MILAN • MADRID
PRAGUE • WARSAW • BUDAPEST • AUCKLAND

Recycling programs
for this product may
not exist in your area.

ISBN-13: 978-0-373-52807-3

HER SINGAPORE FLING

Previously published in the U.K. as RED-HOT RENEGADE

First North American Publication 2011

Copyright © 2010 by Kelly Hunter

Printed in U.S.A.

HER SINGAPORE FLING

CHAPTER ONE

IT WAS all about saving face. From the tailor-made dinner suit and austere white dress shirt he wore, to the antique gold cufflinks at his wrists, to his hard-won air of indifference. Every breath Jake Bennett took this evening was directed towards getting through his brother's engagement party without incident and with honour intact.

'Where's your tie?' murmured his soon-to-be sister-in-law as she stopped beside him, her eyes sharp and her smile wry. 'The one I gave you earlier this evening. The one you're not wearing.'

'In my pocket.' Where it was staying.

Not what Madeline Mercy Delacourte wanted to hear. 'Something wrong with it?' she enquired ever so sweetly.

'Maddy, it's *lilac*.' He liked Madeline. He did. But lately she'd gone a little insane.

'It's lilac for a *reason*, Jacob. Seriously, if you looked any more formidable this evening I wouldn't have any guests left.'

'Well, I try,' he murmured. 'And stop trying to corrupt my apprentice.'

'Po?' Maddy's eyes narrowed with concern. 'What's he done?'

'You want to know what I found in the dojo showers this afternoon?'

'Xena warrior princess?'

'Soap.'

'The horror.'

'*Lavender* soap. Little squares of it, imprinted with fat naked cherubs. Have you *any* idea what sort of message soap like that sends a class full of black belts?' A snigger from Madeline. Clearly she did. Clearly Jake's formidable façade needed work. 'Po said he got them from *you*.'

A peal of laughter this time. 'Sorry,' murmured Madeline once she'd managed to collect herself. 'Have you enlightened Po as to the soap's unsuitability for that particular bastion of rampant masculinity?'

'I thought you might have a word with him.'

'What? And deny you the opportunity? What sort of future sister-in-law would I be if I did that?'

'A helpful one?'

'That's me,' she said. 'I'm all about the help. Tell you what. You manage a smile in the next twenty minutes and I'll find Po and talk soap. Deal?'

'Deal,' he said and smiled.

'Damn,' she said, and Jake's smile widened.

Shooting him a decidedly dirty glare, Madeline swanned off to mingle with the elegant throng gathered in the glittering cocktail bar of Singapore's Delacourte Hotel.

That Madeline and Luke's engagement needed to be celebrated in such moneyed style was a function of Madeline's insane wealth and of a society that expected such an introduction to her betrothed as their due. The proud presentation of family, the underlying tow of big business, and, most importantly, the forging of profitable alliances—all would take place here tonight. Singapore demanded no less of its inhabitants and, for the chance to do business and grow rich here, Singaporeans willingly paid the price.

As far as the proud presentation of family was concerned, the Bennett siblings and their partners were here en masse. Tristan and Erin had flown in from Sydney. Hallie and Nick and their month-old daughter had arrived this morning from London. Serena and Pete had flown in from Greece early afternoon and hit the ground running. Serena was currently immersed in the crowd somewhere. As for Pete, he'd just moved silently into position at Jake's side.

Did they think he hadn't *noticed* the way they were shielding him? The way they'd taken it in turns to keep him company all evening? Monitoring his mindset and his attitude and heaven knew what else. *Fussing* over him, as if he couldn't be trusted to take care of himself?

It was enough to give a man a stabbing headache.

'Look,' he said to Pete as another ripple in the evening air announced the arrival of yet more guests to the party. 'I'm fine. Everything's under control. She's not even here.'

'Nice if you were right,' said Pete with a heavy sigh. 'But you're not. Jianne's just arrived, along with her aunt and uncle if Luke's description of them is anything to go by.'

Jianne's aunt being married to Madeline's most powerful business partner.

Jianne having recently settled in Singapore and Madeline having met her and taken a liking to her.

Jianne Xang-Bennett.

Jake's estranged wife.

'You want a beer?' asked Pete.

'No.'

'Something stronger?'

'Later.' A prickling sensation at the back of his neck almost caused Jake to turn around and see for himself what twelve years' worth of living apart had wrought in his *wife*, but he resisted the notion as he'd resisted the thought of alcoholic fortification and endured the sensation of being observed as best he could.

Pete nodded unsmilingly, his piercing blue gaze stabbing across Jake's shoulder. 'She's seen us.'

This was not news.

'Madeline's herding her towards Hallie and the baby,' continued Pete as the prickling sensation at the back of Jake's neck subsided and silvery laughter graced the room. 'What is it with women and babies?'

'Says the man whose niece had to be prised from his arms earlier this evening a full hour after she'd fallen asleep.'

'Hey, just because she fell asleep on me and not you,' said Pete. 'Face it, you haven't got the touch. Besides, it was my turn.' More of that deliciously female laughter sounded in the background. 'Jianne's becoming better acquainted with our niece. Her niece too, come to think of it. You probably don't want to look.'

'You're probably right.' But Jake did turn and look, and cursed himself for his weakness as the image of an older, breathtakingly beautiful Jianne arrowed into his brain.

She was still the most beautiful woman he'd ever seen. Flawless skin, with an abundance of glossy black hair piled high on her head, Jianne had been built slender and carried with her an air of innocent sweetness that Jake had worked hard to forget. Beauty aside, Jianne Xang had also been born into a family whose personal wealth surpassed that of small countries. A minor detail she'd neglected to mention until after they were married.

Not that he was resentful or anything.

It was just that had he *known* her background he'd have thought twice before asking her to share his common life. Too sheltered for the household full of motherless half-wild siblings that had been in Jake's care. Too gentle to cope with the rawness of their emotions and his. They'd broken her.

He'd broken her.

It was a wonder she'd stayed as long as she had.

It wasn't curiosity that made Jake keep watching her. Curiosity was a mild emotion, easily mastered. This need to drink down every tiny detail of Jianne's appearance clawed at him with the strength of hauntings too long denied.

Jake watched in silence as baby Layla waved tiny fists at Jianne from the safety of her mother's embrace. Jianne's rosebud lips curved. Hallie said something and Jianne looked up, startled, and shook her head. No. Whatever the question, the answer was no.

He wanted to look away. He *would* look away. Soon.

And then Jianne turned her head and looked straight at him through the eyes of an enchantress. Dark as night and deeper than oceans, the western tilt to them a legacy from a great-grandmother who'd been half British on the outside, but on the inside wholly Chinese. Just like Jianne.

Jianne's smile faltered. Jake couldn't even begin to summon his.

He was only vaguely aware that beside him one brother growled beneath his breath, and that across the room another had stilled.

And then Luke stepped into the line of sight between them, bearing orange juice for Hallie and champagne for his guest. Attentive host or the first line of defence? Jake didn't much care. The manoeuvre allowed him to breathe and regroup and smile tightly at Pete, who refused to smile back.

How long would he have to endure this party now that Jianne and her family had arrived? Fifteen minutes? Half an hour? Because he didn't belong here in this rarefied world of extreme wealth and ever so polite society. He suffered it, that was all, while the beast inside him paced its cage and craved escape.

He looked to the vast wall of floor-to-ceiling windows, wishing for wings and for freedom from duty. He looked for a service entrance, another way out, though he knew he wouldn't take it.

He needed to get this over with. Meeting Jianne. Conversing with her. A polite 'how are you'—nothing less would do. An honest 'you're looking well'. Small talk about the weather. Something. Anything. And then he'd ask her the question that had taken hold of him and wouldn't let go until he got an answer.

'I told Madeline and Hallie that this was never going to work,' said Pete from his post at Jake's side. 'I argued this not insignificant point at length but did they listen? No.'

'I'm fine,' said Jake, squaring his shoulders as the prickling sensation between his shoulders beleaguered him once more. 'Everything's fine.'

Pete scowled his dissent. But he said no more.

They were all of them here—the Bennett siblings Jianne had once tried to nurture as if they were her own. Every last one of them, here in this room. Jianne had hoped, had *clung* to the hope, that time and maturity on her part would lessen the daunting impact they had on her, but that wasn't to be. Jianne watched them exchange glances at the sight of her. She watched them move to protect what was theirs.

Jacob, the centre. The heart of this family. The strength, first son.

First love.

The man she'd once given her body to and with it her heart and her soul.

Jacob, with his back turned towards her.

Current husband, a dozen years estranged.

They didn't know, no one knew, how hard it was to put one foot in front of the other and enter that room with her composure in place. Timid rabbits had no place in a room full of watchful waiting tigers. Not if they wanted to survive.

I'm not a rabbit. *Not* a rabbit. Jianne closed her eyes and let the silent litany wash through her before opening her eyes again and pasting a smile on her face as her aunt and uncle moved to her side and Madeline came forward to greet them. Madeline welcomed Jianne's aunt and uncle first, hierarchy understood and respect given, before turning to Jianne and drawing her into a perfumed embrace.

'You look stunning,' said Madeline approvingly.

'Thank you.' The strapless floor-length ivory and blood-red gown, made from the finest silk, was a gown meant for extroverts, not wallflowers. The saleswoman had assured her that the wearing of such a gown would give Jianne all the confidence she needed and more, no matter how awkward the social encounter. The sales-woman had been dead wrong. 'I shouldn't have come,' murmured Jianne. 'This wasn't a good idea.'

'Stay,' coaxed Madeline softly. 'I happen to think it's a very good idea. Come, I'll introduce you to the newest Bennett warrior. The Bennett uncles are still in shock.' Smiles came easily to Madeline these days, and Jianne made an effort to respond in kind. 'It's a girl.'

Baby Layla was a tiny darling with sapphire-blue eyes, alabaster skin, and a shock of auburn hair. Hard to stay distant when a baby smiled a toothless smile and promptly filled her mouth with her fist.

'Layla, this is your auntie Jianne,' said Hallie with a courtesy Jianne hadn't expected. And to Ji, 'Would you like to hold her?'

'Me?' Jianne blinked. 'Yes! I mean, no! I mean... what if she cries? That wouldn't be good.' A vision of her cradling a wailing Layla while all around her wrathful Bennett uncles closed in on them was not an image she wanted to make reality. 'Your brothers would descend.'

'They wouldn't dare,' said Hallie, shooting at least two of them a warning glare. 'They promised me their best behaviour this evening and there are wives enough here to ensure it.'

The notion that those wild-edged Bennett boys had finally allowed themselves to be tamed held a great deal of appeal for Jianne, but as she glanced away from baby Layla and scanned the room she figured Hallie's statement for optimism rather than reality.

Tristan watched her coolly from his position by the window. Pete stood beside Jacob, his expression grim. As for Jake…Jacob wasn't looking her way at all, and because of it Jianne allowed her gaze to linger.

Jacob's suit clung to broad shoulders, powerful legs, and a lean and elegant torso—a testament to the glories of dedicating oneself to the martial arts. His hair was still thick and black and cropped shorter than ever. The lines and planes of his profile had grown sharper but it was still a face to put angels to shame.

From him came an almost visible aura of raw power kept on an incredibly tight leash. Undiluted power had always been an intrinsic part of Jacob's make-up.

The leash was new.

She looked away, just for a moment, just to regroup, and when she looked back Jacob's gaze clashed with hers, those vivid blue eyes of his coldly dismissive and his face set and stern. Jianne stilled, a rabbit caught in a hunter's crosshairs. She wasn't wanted here. She didn't belong here. She'd been wrong to come.

'Stay.' A broad-shouldered man stepped in front of her and broke her eye contact with Jacob. Luke Bennett,

Madeline's intended, those golden eyes of his warmly encouraging as he handed her a glass of champagne. 'Please.'

'Please,' echoed Hallie anxiously. 'Jake needs to see you again. He does. He just…he doesn't quite know it yet.'

'Perhaps you could give me a call when he does,' said Jianne with a strained smile. 'I really don't see what a forced meeting will achieve. Not harmony.'

'Harmony's overrated,' said Luke. 'Occasionally it's best just to step back and let it all explode.'

'Luke defuses bombs,' said Hallie by way of explanation. 'Or not.'

'I'm sure you know what you're doing,' Jianne told Luke politely. 'Just as I'm sure you know what happens to those at the centre of such explosions.'

'We can protect you,' said Luke.

'I don't doubt it.' Certainty enveloped her and firmed her footing. Here at last in this place that glowed with new life and promise was old familiar ground. 'But you won't.' They'd act instinctively to shield the one they loved. They'd shield Jacob. And Jianne would bleed.

'Trust us,' said Luke.

But Jianne was no longer the hopeful young bride who'd once thought she could shower love on a wild and broken family and receive love in return. 'Trust must be earned,' she countered quietly.

'All right, don't trust us.' Grim determination replaced Luke's earlier encouragement. 'But stay, and watch us do everything we can to make you feel welcome here this evening.'

Jianne stayed, and before half an hour had passed Tristan had greeted her and introduced her to his wife,

Pete had done the same, and the small Chinese youth in the smart western suit, who seemed to be being passed around from Bennett to Bennett, had found his way to her side.

'Hello,' she offered warily.

After careful appraisal the boy decided to speak. 'I'm Po. The sensei's apprentice,' he said in flawless Cantonese. When she didn't reply at once he repeated his introduction in Mandarin.

'Which sensei would that be?' Jianne chose English as her language of reply and the boy did not disappoint.

'Sensei Jake.' And when again she didn't reply immediately, 'Bennett.'

'And does Sensei Jake Bennett also teach you English?'

'I know it already,' said Po. 'And Tamul. And some Malay.'

'I'm impressed. How do you come to be fluent in so many languages?'

Just like that the boy's openness disappeared. 'I just do.'

'Well, then.' She offered up a smile. 'Hello, Po. I'm Jianne.'

'Hello.' Fathomless black eyes regarded her steadily. 'You're prettier than your picture.'

'Thank you.' Coherent thought followed the automatic reply. 'What picture?'

The light from a nearby lamp dimmed as someone moved into place beside her. Jianne knew before she looked up that Jacob had joined them, a silent brooding presence bringing new tension to her already overloaded senses.

'Hello, Jacob,' she offered, and if her voice shook, and her insides trembled, well, it was only to be expected. He always had been able to unnerve her. 'I've been making the acquaintance of your apprentice.'

'So I see.' Jacob turned his gaze on the boy. 'What picture?' he echoed grimly.

Po hesitated as if caught between devil and demon. Jake's gaze hardened. 'Po?'

'The one in your wallet.'

'You've been in my wallet?'

'I didn't steal anything,' the boy said hurriedly. 'It was ages ago. The day I came to the dojo. I—' The boy stuttered his way to silence beneath the weight of his sensei's glacial glare. 'I wanted to know more. About you. Wallets are good for that.'

Boy and man stared at one another in fraught silence.

'You dishonour me,' said Jacob finally, in a flat, measured voice.

With a stricken glance for Jianne, Po bolted into the crowd. Jianne stared after him, wishing she could do the same.

'He's yours?' she asked tentatively.

'After a fashion.'

Not Jacob's by blood for the boy was wholly Chinese, but there were plenty of other ways a child could become a man's responsibility. Po's mother could be dead. Jacob could have been seeing her, *living* with her even, and then when she died…and in the absence of other relatives…responsibility for Po could have fallen to him.

'How?'

'Ask Madeline.'

Hardly a comprehensive answer. 'Will you punish him?'

Jacob's lips tightened. 'He took my wallet and went through it. He deliberately invaded my privacy. You don't think he should be disciplined for that?'

'Yes, but…Jacob, he's just a child.'

'What? No beating him?' The deadly edge in Jake's voice flayed her. She couldn't speak. She couldn't breathe. Jianne ducked her head and stared blindly at her champagne glass.

'For heaven's sake, Jianne, I've never raised a hand to either a child or to you and I don't intend to start now. So why don't you just drink your champagne and stop behaving as if I'm about to crucify you? I'm not. I won't. And the sooner you and everyone else watching us realises that, the better.'

Jianne lifted her glass to her lips and sipped. It seemed as good a suggestion as any. Another sip and her champagne half gone while she tried to think of a way to rescue a conversation that had plunged to hell with effortless inevitability.

'You look well,' she offered. Nothing but the truth. 'More formidable than ever.'

'Was that a compliment?'

'I meant it as one.'

'I don't think it was a compliment.'

More champagne seemed as valid a response as any. 'Congratulations on your successes,' she said next. 'The world titles. The master classes. Madeline tells me students come from all over the world to learn from you.'

'You hate karate.'

No, she'd hated the time he'd dedicated to karate. She hadn't realised that, for some, karate was a way of life that bordered on religion or that without it there would have been no way for Jake to restrain the fire that raged inside him. 'I don't hate it. I just never quite understood it. There's a difference.'

'And do you understand it now?'

'A little.' For what it was worth. Nowhere for this topic of conversation to go but downhill so she tried another tack. 'Madeline and Luke seem well suited.'

'They are.'

'And your other brothers…and Hallie…They all seem so civilised now. You did a good job with them.'

'It wasn't my doing.'

Well, it certainly hadn't been hers. She dragged her gaze away from Jake and scanned the room. So many eyes upon them. Not one person inclined to join them.

'Excuse me,' she said after an eternity of silence. 'I think my aunt's looking for me.' She started to walk away.

'Wait,' he said gruffly.

One word, with nothing to follow, but she stayed her ground and waited. Obedience or curiosity? Courage or self-destruction? She did not know.

'How are you enjoying Singapore? Are you settling in?'

That was his question? He'd held her back for *that*? 'Singapore's lovely,' she said warily. 'And I'm settling in well enough.'

'Your aunt told Luke that you had an unwanted suitor.'

Her aunt talked too much.

'She implied that he's pressuring you into considering his offer of marriage.'

'Jacob, I really don't see how this is any of your business.'

'You don't? How very blind of you. *Wife*.' His voice was soft and measured and fooled her not. Beneath the surface calm Jacob Bennett simmered.

'Thing is, I've only heard from others that you have no interest in marrying this man. Maybe you do want to marry again. Maybe I'm just standing in your way.' Jacob looked down at her with those arctic eyes. 'Do you want a divorce?'

'No!' Her reply came too fast, too frightened. While the estranged husband she'd never quite managed to cut from her heart watched her through narrowed eyes. 'I mean…Do you? Po's mother—'

'Is a woman I've never met and Po never mentions. Po's a pickpocket, one of Madeline's strays. She brought him to the dojo so that he'd at least have a roof over his head and a skill to learn.'

'Oh.' Po mystery solved, with Jianne none the wiser about Jacob's current romantic entanglements.

'Your aunt seems to think that if this man doesn't get what he wants, he could become a danger to you,' continued Jake. 'Madeline thinks the same. They're concerned for your safety.'

'They really shouldn't worry so much.' Jianne had done enough worrying these past few months for all of them.

'Has he followed you to Singapore yet?'

'I haven't seen him here.' Yet. No need to burden her husband in name only with the knowledge that Zhi Fu had indeed tracked her down. That the unwanted gifts just kept coming.

'Jianne, is this man a danger to you?'

'In all honesty, I don't know. He never does anything *wrong*.' Frustration had crept into her voice, she knew it had, and she tried to bring her demeanour back to even. 'He plays games, that's all.'

'What kind of games?'

But Jianne had said far too much already. 'It doesn't matter.'

'Mind games?' Quiet. Lethal.

'Jacob, this isn't your fight.'

'You don't think that it's up to me to protect my wife from a stalker?'

'Estranged wife,' she said softly. 'Twelve years estranged.'

Jacob's lips twisted bitterly. 'So you want the protection my name affords you and nothing else. Nothing else from me.'

It sounded so wrong when he put it like that but that was exactly what she wanted. She'd thought, hoped, that everything could stay the same and that their travesty of a marriage could continue on as before. She hadn't once considered Jacob's needs. 'Jacob, if you want a divorce just…get one. If there's someone else…'

He stared at her broodingly. 'What would your unwanted paramour do if he knew you were free of me?'

'I don't know. It doesn't matter. Whatever it is, I'll deal with it. If you want a divorce, do it. You shouldn't have to consider my needs in this.'

'You know, one of these days, Jianne, you're going to realise that martyrdom isn't what people want from you,' he said with quiet viciousness. 'That it's perfectly okay to state your needs and expect them to be considered.'

'Okay, then.' She took a steadying breath and stated her needs straight. 'I do need to stop Zhi Fu's pursuit of me. Coming to Singapore has helped with that. I'm staying with my aunt and uncle, and they're not inclined to encourage his pursuit. He'll not have the access to me here that he had in Shanghai. He'll tire of his games soon.' *Surely* he would tire of his games soon. 'And I'll be free of him.'

Jake stared at her broodingly.

'Jake, I'd rather not involve you. Not unless I absolutely have to.'

He didn't like that. He jammed his hands deep in the pockets of his dress trousers, ruining the line of his suit or enhancing it, depending on one's preference. He looked away, to the window. He looked anywhere but at her. 'Will you at least call *someone* if you think you're in danger and need help?' he said finally.

'I will. I have my cousins and my uncle to call on. Maybe even Madeline or Luke. But I'd rather not call you. Surely you can see why it can't be you?'

'Because I'm as unwanted as he is?'

'What? No! For pity's sake, Jacob. You and Zhi Fu are *nothing* alike. Him, I don't want at all, whereas you…you I once wanted too much.' It was hard to admit that. Her failings. Her flaws. But he deserved that courtesy from her, this husband who asked if she was in danger.

'Do you think I can't protect you?' he said next.

'Have you always been this self-effacing?'

'It's new,' he said grimly. 'I hope to hell it's temporary.'

'I've seen you fight to save your family, Jacob. I've experienced firsthand what you can do, and *will* do, to protect the people in your care. I *know* you'd protect me if I asked it of you.'

'But you won't ask.' He looked at her then and she gathered her courage and held his gaze. Timid rabbit, staring down the tiger.

'I can't.'

'Why not?' Always such absolute focus on the issue at hand or the person he was with. When he'd taken her in his arms and made love to her, ecstasy had rained down on them from the heavens. And when his attention had shifted to other responsibilities, Jianne's demons had surfaced and demanded their due. Obsessive love was like that. Incandescent. Unforgettable. And ultimately destructive. 'Jianne, I need a reason. Why won't you let me help you?'

'How? By pretending to be the happily reunited couple? By bringing you back into my life again until Zhi Fu goes away?'

'If that's what it takes,' said Jake. 'We could set boundaries.'

Jianne smiled mirthlessly. 'So we could.' And she would break them. 'Have you ever been so addicted to something that it nearly destroyed you to give it up?' she asked gently. She held his gaze. He didn't hold hers.

'Yes,' he finally muttered.

'So have I.'

This time when she moved away he made no move to stop her.

CHAPTER TWO

JIANNE managed her goodbyes to Madeline and Luke well enough. She offered up a wistful smile for a sleeping baby Layla and deftly sidestepped Hallie's invitation to lunch the next day. She told her aunt and uncle that she was heading home and watched with affection as her uncle phoned his driver and arranged for her collection. Uncle Yi was taking no chances with her safety—not on his watch—and for once she didn't mind his protectiveness.

A half-grown boy in a carefully pressed suit stood in the shadows cast by hotel towers as Jianne made her way to the waiting car. She slowed her steps until finally she came to a stop beside him. 'Not a party person?' she queried gently.

Po shook his head to signal no, his gaze not leaving her face. Looking for something, wanting something from her, but what? She'd never been good with children. Jake's younger brothers and sister could attest to that. 'I'm sorry our conversation got you into trouble.'

Anguish flickered briefly in Po's dark eyes. 'Me too.'

'Is this the first time you've dishonoured him?' Him being Jacob, stern sensei and keeper of strays. Would-be protector of the weak.

'No,' said Po. 'When it comes to honour and what it is, sometimes I don't get it.'

'What *do* you get?'

The boy considered her question for a very long time. 'Need.'

'Then you and I are more alike than you know.' Jianne offered up a smile, one needy soul to another. 'It's been a pleasure making your acquaintance, Po from the dojo. If ever you have need of me, look me up. Madeline knows where to find me.'

'What if Jake needs you?'

'Po…' How to tell a child something she'd never before put voice to. 'Jake's always known where to find me.'

With a dignity born of desperation, Jianne Xang-Bennett took her leave.

Five minutes after Jianne took her leave from the party, Jake took his. Finding Po took some doing for the kid had skipped out of the hotel. Not far. Not Bugis Street or any of the boy's old haunts. Instead Po had taken refuge in the shadows a few steps beyond the glamorous hotel façade. Tolerated by the hotel doorman because of his smart suit and his shiny black shoes. Mistrusted by the doorman because of those all-seeing eyes.

Hotel staff had fetched Jake's ride up from the hotel's underground parking area. Too much horsepower for practical purposes. Too few opportunities here in Singapore to let speed have its way. Two helmets, the smaller one recently purchased. And a boy who watched him through desolate black eyes. 'You coming?' he asked and held out the kid's helmet.

'Am I still your apprentice?'

'Do you still want to learn karate?'

The boy nodded jerkily.

'Then here's the deal. You steal, you're gone. You make other mistakes, you get one warning about them. Go through anyone's private possessions again and you're gone. Are we clear?'

Another nod.

'Then get on.'

The boy clung on tightly all the way home. And when Jake hit the training floor around two a.m., unable to sleep and needing to work off the tension that came of dredging up old memories best forgotten, a half-grown shadow joined him.

Brothers were useful at times. Jake hadn't expected to see Luke at the dojo the day after Luke's engagement party. He certainly hadn't expected to see Luke waltzing into the dojo at six-thirty a.m., daisy fresh and whistling cheerfully.

'What time did the party finish?' asked Jake.

'Two-ish.'

'So you're here this morning *why*? Maddy kick you out?'

'Madeline opted for Tai Chi by way of morning exercise.' Luke yawned hugely. 'Me, I'm looking for something with a little more kick. It occurred to me that I knew exactly where to find it. You good for a little one on one?'

Jake smiled, slow and sure. 'I guess I could indulge you.' No holding back with brothers the way he held back with students. Blood bond between brothers and unspoken comprehension of intent. A man might spar for exercise or to perfect his warrior's art. A man might spar to compete and to win. Sometimes a man sparred in order to tame the beast inside him. And sometimes he fought to forget.

This morning, Jake was all about the forgetting.

'So how'd it go?' said Luke as he shed his T-shirt and shoes and waited for Jake to do the same. Bare chests, bare fists, black cotton trousers, and neither of them giving a damn about the colour of their belts.

'How'd what go?'

'Last night. Seeing Jianne again.'

'About as well as expected.'

Luke rolled his shoulders. Worked his way into a stretch. 'You talked for long enough.'

'You here to fight or to gossip?'

'Either. Both. Whatever. I'm here for you, precious. Never forget that.'

Jake favoured his brother with a smile a smart man would have been wary of. 'When's the wedding, again?'

'Three weeks.'

'I'll try not to mark you up.' Jake let his fist connect with Luke's unprotected jaw. 'Much.'

Luke countered with a knee to Jake's groin and followed up with an elbow that would have taken a rib out had it connected. Game on, with Luke's reckless smile signalling that if Jake wanted to play by nobody's rules, Luke was perfectly happy to comply.

They fought with fury and catlike grace. Jake had the edge when it came to technique but Luke had a knack for delivering the unpredictable. They both had a generous supply of killer instinct. It was exactly the kind of mindless pleasure Jake needed to take his mind off the living, breathing ghost that was Ji.

It was always going to end in bruises. Jake's meeting with Jianne. This bout with his brother. They hit the floor hard, no mats for the wicked, and Luke groaned and Jake saw stars on the ceiling that he was pretty sure hadn't been there earlier.

'Are you going to look out for her?' asked Luke as he fought free and staggered to his feet.

'She doesn't want me to.' Jake didn't bother to get up, just kicked out with his leg and took Luke down again with ridiculous ease. 'Why do you *never* guard the backs of your knees?'

'Because I like looking at your ceiling.' This time Luke did not get up.

'Hnh.' Jake attempted to rise and decided against it.

'I think you should watch out for her,' said Luke.

'She doesn't want me to.'

'Yeah, like that's ever stopped you.'

'You're family. It was my *job*.'

'And Jianne's not family? So you'll be divorcing her, then?'

Jake had his knee to Luke's chest and his hand to Luke's throat before his brother had time to draw breath.

'Guess not.' Luke's words emerged breathless and strangled.

Jake loosened his grip, and staggered to his feet. He held out his hand to help his brother from the floor. 'Sorry about that.'

'It's fine,' murmured Luke hoarsely as Jake hauled him to his feet. 'I'm fine. Are we done yet?'

'Yes. You staying for breakfast?'

'Only if it comes with painkillers.'

'Wimp.' As they hobbled towards the door.

'Moron.'

Jake slid his brother a sideways glance. 'That bruise on your cheek is never going to clear in time for your wedding.'

'Dimwit,' muttered Luke. 'Idiot.' And after a couple more shuffles towards the door, 'So you'll be seeing her again, then. Calling her. Asking her along to some highbrow show or charity do?'

'She'll never agree.'

'Not if you don't ask. Maybe I'll get Maddy to call Jianne this morning,' said Luke as they hobbled towards the kitchen. 'See if she's had any unexpected callers. Or gifts. Jianne's suitor's big on gifts, according to Maddy. A week ago he sent Ji a wedding dress. Custom made by some fancy fashion house to her exact measurements. She sent it back to him by courier.'

'He sent her a *wedding* dress?'

'It gets better,' said Luke. 'The courier company said they couldn't deliver it because they were told that no one of that name lived at that address. Ji checked with friends in Shanghai. Her gift giver hasn't moved house. But the dress is back with her because the courier company is no longer willing to deliver it. Ji's uncle reckons he's going to hand deliver it. He's currently debating whether to slice it to pieces first.'

'What's to debate?' rasped Jake. 'The size of the scissors?'

Luke smiled ever so slightly. Jake scowled and turned to the fixing of breakfast. 'Jianne doesn't *want* my help. Besides, her uncle's looking out for her. So's Madeline. And so are you. What more does she need?'

Luke reached for a couple of mismatched coffee cups and the tin of instant coffee. 'Some would say you.'

Luke headed out of the dojo some time after nine, fully fed and limping only a little. Jake closed up behind him, for the dojo was closed to the public on Sundays. Nothing to do with prayer and everything to do with rest and retreat and time he could call his own. The dojo phone rang not ten minutes later. Hallie trying to organise a Sunday evening meal for the Bennett clan before everyone headed off to their various destinations the following day. Then it was Madeline on the phone arranging an impromptu lunch at her place. When the phone rang for the third time Jake glared at it and almost didn't pick up, but Tris and Pete were around too and they hadn't checked in yet this morning and like as not they would.

Jake loved his siblings, unconditionally and always, but when everyone got together it reminded him of days long gone when his first priority had been to *keep* them together and inevitably his thoughts would turn to Jianne and then the guilt would kick in that he should have done more, that he *could* have done more to help her fit into the chaos that had been his life.

When he picked up the phone and Jianne said hello he almost dropped it. When she said hello again because he still hadn't spoken he put his fingers to his temple and summoned a reply. 'Are you in trouble?'

'Is that a regular greeting for you?' came the softly spoken reply.

'Regular enough.'

'What's the usual answer?'

'It's usually a variation on "I've met this woman and she's messing with my head."'

'Well, I haven't met this woman,' said Jianne, and lapsed into silence.

'Where are you?' he asked. 'Are you safe?'

'I'm outside your dojo,' she said, with a quiet dignity that only Jianne could wield. 'And I'd like to come in.'

He was at the door within moments, opening it and stepping back to allow her entry, glancing past her to see what trouble might have followed in her wake, but the street was quiet, and the faces on it familiar ones. He shut the door behind her and turned around warily.

She looked breathtaking in a lemon coloured sundress that fell in soft waves to her knees. Her hair had been pulled back from her face with ebony combs, and she clutched her handbag in front of her like a shield.

He gestured for her to precede him through the entrance foyer and on into the training hall, and closed his eyes and prayed for mercy when he saw the length of her hair. She'd kept it long, a glossy rippling river than ran almost to the base of her spine. Once upon a time, Jianne's hair had framed their lovemaking like a silken shroud. It still would.

His body approved of the notion, even as his mind shied away from it. *Surely* he'd learned his lesson the last time Jianne had come into his life? Some things were simply too fragile for a man like him to touch.

'What did he do?' he said harshly, bringing his thoughts back to now and the possible reasons for Jianne's visit. 'Your unwanted beau.'

'How do you know that's why I'm here?' she said as he walked her through the training hall and out into the tiny kitchen area. He didn't have a sitting room. He didn't have a rec room either. Just a few sparsely furnished bedrooms out back for occasional guests and visiting students, and a loftlike crib of his own above the training hall.

'Why else would you be here?' he countered. 'Last night you considered my company the greater of two evils. This morning, here you are. The balance has changed and I didn't tip it. So what did he do?'

'You always tip the balance, Jacob. It's what you do.' She looked at the shabby table and chairs and remained standing.

'You want to sit?' he offered, belatedly remembering Jianne's reliance on protocols and manners and his general lack of them. 'Something to drink?'

Jianne sat at his shabby Formica table. She decided against refreshment. Jake crossed his arms, leaned against the counter and waited.

'He's here,' she said quietly. 'Zhi Fu. An invitation arrived from him this morning to his house party here in Singapore.'

'So he followed you.' Jake didn't like this latest development but, given the man's obsession with Jianne, he wasn't overly surprised. 'You had to have known it was a possibility.'

'I had hoped Zhi's business ties would prevent it,' she murmured. 'I was counting on it.'

'So what now?' he asked somewhat more gently.

Jianne shook her head. 'I don't know. I was going to refuse his invitation, I always refuse his invitations, but then my uncle suggested that a stronger message might be warranted. He suggested I attend Zhi's housewarming party. With you.'

'Aggressive,' murmured Jake. 'I like it.'

A tiny smile from Jianne. 'You would.'

'Was that a compliment?' he asked silkily. 'I don't think it was.'

'Suit yourself,' she murmured. 'The thing is I find myself in need of a protector. A Shaolin in the purest sense, and I've only ever come across one of those in my lifetime. You. Zhi Fu's here in Singapore. He's renting the home directly across the road from my aunt and uncle's house. He'll be able to monitor my every move, just as he did back in Shanghai.'

Protectiveness kicked in hard, and with it a cold hard rage at the man's predatory behaviour.

'My uncle thinks that getting my own place in some other part of Singapore would be unwise,' continued Jianne. 'He thinks Zhi Fu would follow.'

'Your uncle's probably right.' Jake eyed her steadily, noting the shadows beneath her eyes, and trying not to notice the curve of her cheek or those crushed rosebud lips. 'Have you considered taking out a restraining order on him?'

'He'd have to threaten me before I could do that. As I said last night, he never does anything *wrong*. Not in the eyes of the law.' Jianne gave a weary shrug, her expression beyond bleak. 'You don't know what he's like. He's very very good at winning people over to his way of thinking.

He'll be charming and helpful and invoke guanxi and then they'll be his. That's what he does. It's how he wins. He gives people nowhere else to go but to him.'

'How long has this been going on?' She didn't answer. 'Jianne?' he said more gently.

'Five years,' she said, with an alarming tremor in her voice. 'It took a while for me to realise what he was doing and how he was doing it. My father called me crazy at first, and then he too got caught up in Zhi Fu's web. My father doesn't think I'm crazy any more, only now there's nothing he can do about it. I'm so *sick* of there being nothing anyone can do about it. I want my life back. I want to fight this.' Her chin rose stubbornly. 'I want to win.'

'What do you want from me, Ji? You want me to accompany you to his house party? I'll do it. What else?'

'I want him to think we're in the process of renewing our relationship.' Hot colour stained Jianne's cheeks but she held his gaze. 'I want you to give off signals that we're…that you're…'

'Protective?' he offered gruffly.

'That too.'

Jake Bennett had never considered himself a twice-cursed man. Until now. 'What else?'

'I can't stay at my uncle's any more, knowing Zhi could be watching every move I make. I *can't*.' Twelve years ago Jianne's calm reserve had seemed to run soul deep. Either she'd come out of her shell somewhat over the intervening years or she was deeply spooked by Zhi Fu's latest move. 'I need a place to stay. Somewhere that fits with the overall plan. Somewhere I can feel safe.'

She looked at him then and he knew, he just *knew* what was coming next. 'Oh, no,' he said. 'No,' and ran his hands through his hair for good measure. 'You *can't* be thinking of staying here.'

'Madeline says you have a row of rooms out the back that you put people in.'

'Yes, but...have you *seen* them? We're talking no frills here, Jianne. Not one.'

'I don't need much.'

'No cook, no maid, just me and Po and four or five karate classes a day, starting at six and running through until late. The kid hardly sleeps. Sometimes if I'm awake we'll train during the night. And this is the kitchen. It's also the dining room, lounge room, and Po's study.'

She stared at him steadily.

He couldn't believe she thought this would work. That they could make it work. Escorting her here and there on occasion was one thing, but this... 'Wait till you see the bathrooms.'

'If you don't want me here, just say so,' she said calmly. 'It's a lot to ask of you. An invasion of your privacy that makes going through your wallet look like child's play. I know that. I *will* understand if you say no, Jacob.'

'And if I do say no?' he countered. 'Where will you go?'

She had no answer for that.

'You won't like it here. There's no softness here,' he warned her one last time. 'It's sweaty and hot and noisy and raw. The street is two steps away. It's not a particularly peaceful street.'

'I'll manage.'

He couldn't believe he was even considering her request. Thinking forward to where to put her and how best to protect her. He paced the tiny kitchen with growing agitation. He scowled for good measure. She looked like a fragile fairy-tale princess. Snow White in need of a haven. He, on the other hand, was wearing black track sweats, a ratty grey T-shirt, and he wasn't wearing shoes. Where the hell were a bunch of pickaxe-toting dwarves when you needed them?

'Come with me,' he muttered and led her up a narrow staircase to one side of the training floor, and opened the door to his crib.

It was spacious. Space he had in spades, which was something of a luxury in Singapore. A huge expanse of polished wooden floorboard covering an area the same size as the training hall below. A bed made up with white sheets, a navy-coloured coverlet and a couple of pillows graced the far corner. He'd had a shower and toilet plumbed into the opposite corner, with a half-wall and a makeshift screen providing some semblance of privacy. A highset band of slatted warehouse windows ran the length of both longways walls. He'd covered one of those walls with a row of silk tapestries depicting a battle scene, heavy on the death and destruction. A reading chair, a reading lamp, and a not-quite-straight bookshelf crammed with books completed the tableau. Narrow storage space behind the far wall hid his belongings and his clothes.

'It's still not much but it's better than what's on offer downstairs,' he said curtly.

'But…' Jianne gazed around her in silence and he gritted his teeth at how sparsely furnished his home no doubt looked to her eyes. 'This is your space.'

'I'll clear out. I can stay downstairs.'

'No! There's no need to turn you out of your bed. I never meant to do that. Have me stay downstairs. Whatever's there, it'll do.'

'This is what I'm offering, Jianne. It's the only offer you'll get from me when it comes to accommodation. You, up here, out of the way.'

She hesitated.

'Take it or leave it.' On this he would not bend.

'Okay.' She took a deep breath, as if shoring up her resolve. 'I'll take it. I'll pay rent, of course,' she added hurriedly, and named a weekly rate that would have kept her in six star luxury, not a warehouse bedsit atop a downtown dojo.

'Keep your money,' he grated. 'I don't want it.'

Jianne recoiled as if he'd struck her.

Jake gritted his teeth and prayed for mercy. 'Must you *flinch* every time I look at you?'

'Must you *glare* every time I open my mouth?' she replied in kind. 'People pay rent when they live in a place that's not their own. Why is my offering to do so such an insult to you? Is your pride such an enormous thing that there can be no room for mine?'

Money had been a sore point between them from the moment Jianne had revealed exactly how much of the stuff she had. Tens of millions, probably hundreds of millions by now. A tiny detail she'd waited until six months into their marriage to let slip, when she'd offered to pay for a housekeeper to come in each day and help clean the Bennett family house and prepare healthy meals for a hungry family.

She'd been drowning in household chores she had no idea how to cope with and all Jake had seen was the blow to his pride. The housekeeper hadn't eventuated. Jianne's drowning had continued.

Not the Bennett family's finest moment.

'Fine,' he amended. 'Contribute something to the running of the place if it makes you feel better. A cleaner comes in daily—I can have him do up here too, that's not a problem. But a couple of hundred Sing a week will cover your stay. If you still don't think that's enough, I'll give you an account you can put some money into. It's one I've set up for Po. Put however much you want in there.'

He thought it a fair compromise, the accepting of her money on Po's behalf. Never let it be said that Jacob Bennett didn't learn from his mistakes.

She sent him a long, considering look, before nodding slightly. 'I'll do that.'

Jake could move fast when he wanted to. Ask any opponent he'd ever faced in a championship match. Hell, ask Jianne—their courtship had lasted all of five minutes before he'd put a ring on her finger. Ever since then he'd tried to slow down some and *think* when it came to life-altering decisions. 'Does your uncle know that you want to move in here?'

'He does.'

'And he approves?' Jake had faced Xang family disapproval before. He knew its power. He needed to know on how many fronts he'd have to fight.

'He does. Whatever you need, you'll have his full co-operation.'

'And your father?'

'My father can't help me,' she said flatly.

'Are you *sure* you don't want to think about this some more?'

'If I think about it I won't do it.'

'Doesn't this *tell* you something?' he said in a last-ditch effort to sway her to another—*any* other—course of action.

'Yes.' A faint smile tilted her luscious lips. 'Don't think.'

They agreed, over a scalding-hot cup of tea back in the shabby kitchen, that Jianne would move in later that afternoon. Jake figured, in an 'if I'm going to be damned I may as well burn' kind of way, that Jianne had better accompany him on his lunch and dinner rounds. No way was he leaving her here on her own while he went out. Not going to happen. Not until her unwanted paramour had learned the meaning of the word no.

'I need to go get cleaned up,' he muttered, running a hand over the stubble on his chin for confirmation. 'I'm heading over to Maddy's soon for lunch. You may as well come too. Your uncle can have your belongings delivered there.'

'Who else is going to be at this lunch?' she asked warily.

'Luke and Po. Probably everyone else as well.'

'Everyone, as in all your siblings and their families?'

Jake nodded. 'It's not often we have a chance to get together these days. When we do get the opportunity we take it. Hallie's booked us in somewhere for dinner too. I'll get her to change the reservation to include you.'

'Don't. Please. I really don't want to intrude on your family meals.'

Jake smiled bitterly. Everyone had their little crosses to bear. His siblings had always been one of Jianne's. 'I know what you think of them, Jianne. That they're too wilful, too bent on trouble, too unrestrained. But that was then and this is now and I'm proud of them, all of them, and you should know something. In asking for my help, you don't just get me on side, you get them too. Whatever they can do to protect you, whatever needs doing, they'll do it, and that's worth something. You could try being grateful.'

'I am grateful.' She squared her shoulders and held his gaze, something she would never have done twelve years ago. 'But you need to know something too. About your brothers and your sister…and me. There are no unconditional ties of love between us, no bonds of trust or acceptance. If they follow your lead I'll be grateful, but I'll never make the mistake of thinking that they're helping me because they want to. They'll be doing it for you.'

'You're wrong.'

'No.' She sent him a careful smile but the shadows in her eyes spoke of deeper, darker, memories. 'I'm not. I'll come to Madeline's for lunch but I'll not join you all for dinner. I'll stay at my uncle's tonight and sort out a few things I need to sort out like transport and the belongings I want to bring with me. I'll move in tomorrow. That way you can join your family for dinner without thinking you have to be responsible for me, and everyone will be happy.'

The suggestion was quintessentially Jianne and dredged up memories of her making similar suggestions, over and over again during the course of their ill-fated marriage. Forfeiting *her* needs in an attempt to accommodate *his* needs and the needs of his siblings. And they'd let her. Every last one of them, Jake included, had let her do it. 'No,' he said grimly. 'Lunch at Madeline's if you want to, and only if you want to, and then we'll go to your uncle's and get your stuff and then we'll come back here and get you settled. Dinner with my family doesn't have to happen.'

'But—'

'No, Jianne. Just…no,' he said, and glared at her for good measure, before stalking out of the room and making his way to the dojo showers. He stripped down and stepped beneath a measly drizzle of lukewarm water. The spray from the next showerhead wasn't any better. Sighing, he added new showerheads and possibly new plumbing to tomorrow's work list. He shoved his face beneath the spray and rubbed it hard before looking down at his decidedly aroused anatomy.

'No.' The 'no's were coming thick and fast today. 'No way.' He *would* not give into his desire for his lovely and ever so vulnerable wife no matter how much his body urged differently. Get clean. Get dressed. Get Jianne's unwanted suitor off her back and get her out of here. *That* was his plan. And if he could show her in the process that he knew these days how to respond fairly to the needs of those around him, well, so much the better.

This time round Jianne's needs would not come last.

He wouldn't let them.

CHAPTER THREE

MADELINE's luxury penthouse was about as far removed as a person could get from Jake's spartan existence. Madeline's gracious hospitality was legendary and she didn't disappoint when she opened the door to him and Jianne shortly after midday, blinked once, and swung smoothly into a warm and welcoming hostess routine.

Luke stilled when he saw Jianne at Jake's side and so did Hallie. Pete shot him a searching glance. Tristan just watched. Not one of his siblings said a word.

'Jianne's staying at the dojo for a while,' he said to no one in particular, and you could have heard a butterfly breathe in the silence.

Thank heaven for partners. Serena, Pete's wife, swung into action first, smiling and moving and making some kind of small talk that involved Tris's wife, Erin. A gentle reminder that astonishment was no cause for rudeness and that the Bennett siblings needed to lift their game.

'She's nervous,' he said to Madeline as he watched Jianne interact with the other Bennett wives.

'Why wouldn't she be?' countered Madeline. 'With the exception of Serena and Erin—to whom I'm eternally grateful—not one of you knows how to relax around her. What'd she do? Torture puppies?'

Jake glowered at her.

'All right, don't confide in me,' she murmured. 'But if you want my advice on how to make Jianne relax in this company I suggest you look to yourself. If *you* can relax, the rest of them will. Beer or spirits?'

'Beer.'

'Perfect,' she said with a sunny smile. 'I'll go and see if I can tempt Ji to a champagne. And I still think a lilac tie would help *a lot.*'

'Never going to happen.'

'Objection noted.' Madeline sent him a considering look that Jacob had learned to be wary of. 'Fortunately I'm a woman of uncommon inventiveness when it comes to bringing out a man's softer side.' Moments later an angel-faced baby girl had been deposited in his arms and there was nothing for it but to keep on holding her and let Po hover protectively over them both and suffer Madeline eyeing him with evil glee as she headed towards Jianne.

Jianne had been doing all right during those first few minutes of her arrival at Madeline's lunch gathering. Right up until the moment someone had seen fit to deposit baby Layla into her uncle Jacob's arms. Everything started hurting after that.

Watching the husband she'd once loved so fiercely cradle his niece with such gentle authority and fend off all attempts to get him to hand her over scraped at Ji's heart. She'd wanted children once. Not immediately following her whirlwind marriage, but at some stage in her and Jacob's future she'd imagined them. Imagined Jake with them.

She accepted the champagne Madeline handed her and smiled and hid the assault on her heart as best she could. If she wanted to continue this charade she'd have to get used to being in Jake's company again and the company of his siblings. And that meant conversing with them.

Bracing herself, Jianne turned her attention once more to the small knot of people that now included Luke and Tristan as well as Serena and Erin. She summoned a smile and admired the design of the glittering rings on Erin's fingers, and discovered that Erin was a jeweller and had made the rings herself. Small talk between strangers, the kind that made people relax, and it was working, sort of, until Jake and a sleepy baby joined them, and all conversation ceased.

When the silence grew beyond awkward, Tristan pinned her with his golden gaze and asked her if she'd ever managed to finish her visual design degree.

'Yes,' she stammered, startled that he'd even remembered such a thing. 'Yes, I finished it. I make my living nowadays doing design work for various organisations. International companies in need of multilingual branding, mostly.'

'Do you need to make a living?' asked Jake quietly, his blue gaze unreadable. 'What happened to your trust fund?'

'It matured, I reinvested it, and now there's more of it,' she said calmly. 'If you're asking me if I need the money my work brings in the answer's no. If you're asking me if I like to work and imagine that what I do is of value to people, the answer's yes.'

Jacob stared at her through those unreadable eyes, until finally Tristan spoke up again. 'Will you be able to work from Singapore?'

'Easily. I've clients here as well as in Hong Kong and Shanghai. My travelling schedule should stay about the same.'

'Will you need office space?' asked Jake.

'I already have it.'

'Is it secure?' asked Jake.

'Yes, it's in my uncle's office complex.' Baby Layla kicked out with her legs and struck her uncle square in the chest, a blow that made three besotted uncles beam and Jianne's heart bleed a little more for the picture they made.

'Girl's got talent,' said Luke, and shot Jianne a considering glance. 'Would you like to hold her?'

'What?'

'Would you like to hold Layla for a while?' he repeated. 'You're the only one here who hasn't had a turn yet.'

'Okay,' she said faintly, damping down the chaos of her emotions and summoning a polite smile for the benefit of Jacob's family.

Jacob's blue eyes were dark with some unidentifiable emotion. His generous, kissable mouth was set in unsmiling lines. His hands were impossibly gentle as he deposited baby Layla into her arms.

'There's a rule that says whoever's holding her gets to keep her for at least fifteen minutes before handing her on,' he said gruffly. 'Don't let them con you out of your time.'

'I won't.' Jianne smiled down at the sleeping cherub. 'She's so tiny,' she whispered, and smoothed the soft cotton wrap away from Layla's face with the gentlest of fingertips. 'So fragile. I'm scared I'll breathe and break her.'

'So am I,' said Jake, and the agony in his voice had her glancing up at him in concern, only he wasn't there any more, he was already halfway across the room, with Po the boy who saw everything, shooting her a lightning glance before following in his sensei's wake.

The afternoon bled into the evening with a speed Jianne hadn't anticipated. Evening plans swung into place. Po successfully begged a sleepover at Madeline's and taxis were ordered to take everyone to the restaurant. Everyone but Jianne and Jacob.

Hallie had started to protest when Jacob had told her that he wouldn't be joining them for dinner. Jacob had silenced her with a glance and shortly thereafter they'd taken their leave.

A silent taxi ride later and he and Jianne stood beside the darkened dojo door. He unlocked it and ushered her inside, her two bags of luggage slung over his shoulder. He carried the bags upstairs to his room—her room now—and collected up a handful of clothes before telling her he was going to grab some Thai food from the takeaway across the road and for her to come down whenever she was ready.

'Jacob, wait.'

He turned around slowly, his brilliant blue eyes guarded and wary. Jianne tried a tentative smile and his eyes grew warier still. 'I still think you should be up here and I should take one of your other guest rooms.'

'Don't start.' Two words, with a world of quiet warning behind them.

'I'm not a child to be reprimanded, Jacob. I have an opinion. I have a right to state it.'

'You stated it this morning. I told you then that if you wanted to stay, you'd be sleeping up here. It's safer and more comfortable.'

'It's yours.'

'Not any more. Was there anything else?'

Yes. The desire to touch him was all encompassing, even if only to find out just how big a mistake she'd made in coming here. Jianne stepped out of her comfort zone and into Jacob's personal space and watched his magnificent body go predator still. Leashed, in a way she'd never seen him be. 'Thank you for this,' she said. 'For your help.'

'It's nothing.'

'It's not nothing to me. I feel safe here. Safer and stronger than I've felt in a long time.'

'You're taking control of the situation,' he said with the rarest of smiles, a smile just for her. 'Those are just side effects.'

'I still couldn't have done it without you.' She reached out and brushed his hand with hers. She had to know if the all-consuming heat that had once engulfed them was still there beneath his skin, beneath all that daunting self-control.

It was.

Jake trembled beneath her touch, dark lashes dropping down to shield his eyes as he jerked his hand away from hers and stepped back as if stung.

'Don't,' he said raggedly.

Jianne absorbed Jacob's startling response to her touch with a calmness born of desperation. 'It wasn't an invitation to intimacy, Jacob. All I did was touch you.'

'Don't,' he repeated, and this time his eyes blazed with fierce warning. 'Not here. Not when we're alone. I can't.' He turned away and headed for the door as if all the demons of hell were after him.

He shut the door firmly behind him and Jianne let out the breath she'd been holding along with a ragged whimper to accompany it. Jacob had meant his words as a warning. Who knew that they would lodge in her soul as a bright arrow of hope?

She looked around the room lit dimly by the light filtering in through slatted windows. Red neon up one end, stripes of blue hue at the other and not a curtain in sight. Too light for sleeping unless a person was used to it or they got tired enough for light not to matter. On the bright side, there'd be no creeping up on her in the darkness while she slept.

Jianne looked to the bed, Jacob's bed, plainly adorned. The sheets and pillowcases were fresh since this morning and so was the dove-grey coverlet. Jacob's books were in the bookshelf and the leather reading chair held the imprint of his body. The faintest scent of him still lingered in the air, teasing at her senses, conjuring up memories of possession and surrender best forgotten.

Jianne undid her case and set her nightshift on the end of the bed before collecting up her toiletries and making her way to the washroom. Did Jacob still sleep naked? She never had. Not since she'd fled his bed all those years ago.

Shedding her sundress, Jianne stepped beneath the shower spray, closed her eyes and let the water cool her overheated skin. Jacob's warehouse apartment didn't boast the kind of luxury she'd been born to, true enough, but there was a tranquillity here that came of simple needs being met. Shelter, food, discipline and purpose. A warrior's needs. No room for softness, only that wasn't quite true, for there *was* softness in Jacob along with a generous heart and a powerful need to protect those who needed protection.

He'd made room for Po here.

And he'd made room for her.

Amazing what snippets the brain dredged up when memories were allowed to surface. Like Jianne's favourite Thai dish, which Jake figured he might as well order. She liked steamed greens too, so he ordered some of those then his own preference along with enough boiled rice to feed an invading army and then another fish dish for good measure. Jake didn't care that he'd ordered way too much food for two. He needed something to focus on other than the woman he'd once loved beyond measure, and right now food would have to do.

Jake stood outside the shop and waited while they prepared his order, scanning the street for signs of strangers who didn't belong. He knew this neighbourhood, knew the people who lived here. Zhi Fu might try and find purchase here, he might even succeed, but the watcher would be watched and there was more than one way of getting in and out of the dojo unnoticed. Back ways, through alley ways and the shops of people whose businesses bordered his. Po used all of the back ways out of the dojo and had probably invented a few more by now. Po had a thief's dislike of having less than half a dozen exits to choose from.

Jake stared up at the frosted and slatted warehouse windows of his second-floor apartment, trying to gauge how secure *they* were, and whether someone in the building opposite would be able to see in through them.

Not if he slanted the slats the right way.

His order came up so he collected it along with the cook's well wishes for good eating. He crossed the road and headed up the side alley towards his kitchen door entrance this time, rather than the front entrance. The kitchen door was old and the lock a simple one. He'd never had a security system installed. Maybe it was time he did.

Jianne opened the door to him before his key even hit the lock.

'Don't do that,' he said as she stood back to let him in.

'If I wanted to live in a prison I'd have stayed at my uncle's.'

'If you want to live here you'll do as I say.' Jake shut the door behind him and put the food on the table, trying to ignore the scent of freshly washed woman that permeated the air. He did his best not to notice the way Jianne's lightweight skirt and camisole showcased her fragile beauty or the way his pulse kicked at the sight of her. 'Just humour me, Jianne, and check that you know who's at the door before you open it. Especially when you're alone. It's a good habit to get into.'

'I bet it's not one of your habits.'

'I'm not the one being harassed by a stalker.' Jake rummaged about in the kitchen drawer. Chopsticks if she wanted them, spoons and forks if not. Jianne assisted by collecting up soy sauce and salt from the kitchen shelf, and glasses from the drying rack.

'What do you want to drink?' he asked. 'I have beer, Scotch, or water. Or there's a vending machine in the dojo that does sports drinks and high-energy cola. If none of that appeals, there's a supermarket around the corner.'

'Water's fine,' she said. 'Or beer, if you're having one.' So he fished both from the fridge and left it up to her to decide.

He'd forgotten Jianne's knack for bringing order to chaos. For making teenage boys wash their hands before sitting down to eat. For taking quiet pleasure in the setting of a table, never mind that most everyone slated to sit at that table would be far more intent on inhaling their food than taking the time to converse and connect. 'No bowls,' he said as he peered in the cupboard. 'I think Po used the last of them to mix up some furniture polish.'

'For what?' she said, bemused, and true enough he had no wooden furniture in the place that was in any way deserving of polish.

'Po and Luke have been making a study desk for Po's room. The polish was for that. Which means no bowls left, just mismatched plates. It's not what you're used to.'

'Am I complaining?'

'You hardly ever do,' he muttered. 'Makes it hard for people to know what you're thinking. What you want.'

'I'd like the plate with the blue border,' she said in that quiet way of hers that made it impossible to tell if she was teasing, serious, or something in between. 'And I'd like us to sit down and eat.'

That worked for a little while, but eventually conversation had to be made. Politeness demanded it and Jacob tried hard to begin it, never mind that small talk had never been his forte. 'Why Singapore?' he asked.

'My aunt and uncle are here,' said Jianne with a careful glance in his direction. 'Some of my clients are here. And I knew you were here and that it wouldn't hurt for Zhi Fu to think that I might want to see you again.'

'How did you know I was here?'

'My cousins told me,' she said. 'They've always known where you were and what you were doing.'

'How?'

'They Google you.'

'Oh.' Scratch the dastardly private-eye theory. 'Right.'

'World titles attract attention,' she continued with the hint of a smile. 'Did you know you have a fan site? Pictures and all.'

'Can we *not* talk about this?' he murmured. 'Ever?'

Jianne's smile widened at this and she speared a prawn with her chopsticks. 'I never really knew what you wanted to do with your life. Apart from win martial arts tournaments, that is. But teaching suits you, I think.'

'I never really planned to teach,' he told her readily enough. 'I came to this dojo after winning my first world title. I was battle weary and looking for the old sensei to improve my technique. I stayed a week. Three months later I was back. This time I wanted more balance. Whenever I could get away I'd come here and I'd return home…rested. When the old sensei decided to sell up and return to Thailand I decided that this was the life I wanted. The timing was good, my brothers and Hallie weren't kids any more, so I made him an offer.'

'Do you ever miss Australia?'

'No.'

'Do you miss your family?'

'Luke's Singapore based too. The rest of them call in often enough.'

'And your father? Does he call in?'

'Not often, no.'

'Did he ever get over your mother's death?'

'No.'

'Have you ever forgiven him for not standing by you when you needed him?'

'What do you think?'

'I don't know. That's why I asked.' She eyed him solemnly. 'Have you ever forgiven me?'

'Jian—' Jake didn't even know where to start when it came to answering that one. 'I didn't realise what I was asking when I asked you to become part of the Bennett household back then. We didn't give you much support. *I* didn't give you much support. I never blamed you for leaving when you did.'

Much.

Jianne spooned a small serving of greens onto her plate to accompany her equally small portion of prawns. Jake eyed the remaining food on the table.

'You should eat more,' he muttered.

'Why did you agree to help me?' she asked.

'Because you needed it.'

'Any other reason?'

'Maybe I just like to fight.'

'That's not news.'

'Sorry.' Jake managed a half-smile at her not-quite-hidden disgruntlement. Jianne had hated the fighting lifestyle he'd once lived. She'd resented the mental and physical demands it had placed on him and she'd been horrified by his thirst for more. Gentle, nurturing Jianne had never really understood the anger that had raged in him back then or his ferocious need to tame it before it spilled over onto the people he loved. He hadn't had the words to explain it. He didn't have them now. 'Maybe I figured that helping you out would provide me with a new challenge. A different kind of fight from the ones I'm used to. And maybe the general consensus is that I owe you and that it wouldn't have mattered what you asked of me, I'd have done it.'

Jianne's eyes widened at this. She opened her mouth as if to speak but no words came out. She closed her mouth, blinked, and tried again. 'You mean I've had an honour-bound slave at my disposal all these years and nobody thought to mention it?' She looked bemused. 'It's not a scenario I've ever imagined. Certainly not in reference to my relationship with you.' A whisper of a smile tilted her lips. 'Then again, it does have a certain basic appeal.'

'Easy on the enslavement, Empress Wu,' he warned. 'Nothing good ever comes of it.'

'Oh, I don't know. You could be naked but for a loin-cloth,' she murmured. 'There could be oil involved.'

'Not in this lifetime.'

'This slavery thing,' she continued serenely. 'You're the one *obeying* the orders, right? As opposed to giving them?'

Jake speared her with his most intimidating stare and kept right on eating.

'Just checking,' she said. 'I'd hate to get it wrong.'

Jacob wouldn't let Jianne help wash the dinner dishes, though he didn't object to her tidying the table and putting the leftovers in the fridge. His minimalist kitchen meant minimal clean-up afterwards. Jianne could see the appeal. But the tense silence in which he washed those few dishes didn't hold much appeal at all. She'd thought they'd made some progress towards feeling at ease with one another over dinner. Clearly she'd thought wrong. 'Can there be music?' she said.

'There can if you go upstairs. There's a sound system up there.' Not exactly subtle in his attempt to get her to go somewhere he wasn't. 'I've some paperwork to do in my office,' he said next. 'I'll turn in for the night after that.'

'Is there anything you need from upstairs?' she asked politely. 'Clothes? Toiletries?'

'Not tonight. I'll get the rest of the things I need tomorrow while you're at work. You *are* going to work at your office tomorrow. Right?'

'I am.'

The man looked downright relieved to hear it. 'And when's this house-warming party you want me to take you to?'

'Friday.' Five nights away.

'We should go out together before then,' he said with obvious reluctance. 'Somewhere public. See what happens.'

'Okay.' The idea was a sound one. The reality was likely to bite. 'So…goodnight?'

'Yeah.' He nodded and turned away.

Jianne climbed the stairs and closed the door behind her. She looked at Jacob's bed and groaned aloud. Instead of the bed she headed for the bathroom, and brushed her teeth and plaited her hair the better to avoid tangles in it come morning. She approached the bed and changed into her sleepwear. She circled the bed without touching it, trying to choose a side.

Not a soft bed, she thought when she'd finally gathered the courage to slip between the sheets. Jacob's bed, and there was a sensuousness that came of being in it. Stolen pleasure, fierce and forbidden, and she closed her eyes and caught her lip between her teeth and allowed herself to remember a time when the pursuit of ecstasy had ruled her.

She'd been too meek for him everywhere else. Too unsure of her role within Jacob's unruly family. Too unfamiliar with her new way of life to navigate it confidently. Only in the abandon with which they'd surrendered to passion had they proven equal.

In every way.

Sleep would not come. One a.m. Two a.m., and still sleep eluded her and her body's desire for sexual satisfaction grew stronger. She tossed the covers aside and paced the room, bare feet making no sound on the battered wooden floor. Jacob's tapestries were made of silk and the impulse to touch them was one she could indulge. She allowed herself that small pleasure, and that of sitting in Jacob's reading chair, her legs tucked beneath her and her thighs pressed firmly together as she studied the spines of his books.

His scent tantalised her. The need for touch tugged at her. She closed her eyes and rested her head back against Jacob's chair and begged sleep to come and take her away.

She almost managed it. Three a.m. and back in bed, with her breathing slow and easy and her mind shut down tight against the memories of her time in Jacob's arms, she'd almost reached gentle oblivion. Until a faint sound came to her from below, a dull, irregular thudding.

Not noisy pipes. Not the pounding of someone at the door. Something else.

The door did not groan as she opened it. The stairs did not creak beneath her weight. Jianne crept halfway down them the way dusk settled over the day. Silently, stealthily, until finally she could sit on a step and lean forward and peer down into the training hall below.

The light was the same as in the room above. Bands of striped moonlight and neon sneaking in through slatted windows. A man stood with his back to her in the shadowy corner of that room, naked to the waist, loose black trousers riding low on his hips. Desolation and desperation in his rhythmic pounding of flesh against a boxing bag that hung from a ceiling beam. Muscles rippling across his back as his patterns grew more complex and power ripped through him.

Jacob's balance didn't falter. His intention didn't waver. Oblivion through exhaustion. Peace in the wake of destruction. Jianne watched him for long minutes before finally retreating back to the room he'd put her in. She crawled between the bedcovers and closed her eyes as the muffled pounding continued.

But she did not sleep.

CHAPTER FOUR

THE dojo day had well and truly started when Jianne came downstairs at around eight the following morning. Unfortunately the stairs fed down into the training hall below—there was no other way down. Discretion was not an option, but at least she was dressed for the day and not still in her sleepwear.

She wore her usual work attire of grey tailored trousers, high heels, and a sleeveless shirt. Today's shirt was hot pink and she wore her hair in a French roll, the better to present a professional image. It was an image that had no place inside dojo walls and she knew it. So too did Jacob's students, who fell ominously silent, one by one, as she descended the stairs.

Jacob hadn't seen her yet, he was rifling through an equipment trunk with two of his students, and she didn't know whether to interrupt him or not. All she had to do was catch his eye, give him a nod, and walk out of the door. It should have been easy enough to do, but given the way her stay here was progressing even that small interaction had the potential for disaster.

She started across the training-room floor only to halt when Jacob looked up, caught her gaze, and headed towards her. For a man who'd spent half the night pounding on a boxing bag he looked remarkably well rested.

Jianne, on the other hand, had resorted to artifice in order to disguise her sleepless night.

'You're heading off to work?' he asked when he reached her, his voice low and gruff, just one more swipe at a woman's composure. From the loose-limbed way he walked to the broad expanse of his T-shirt-clad shoulders, *everything* about Jacob had been designed to render women sleepless, and right now she resented every bit of it.

Jianne nodded, her throat the tiniest bit dry for words. Nothing a cup of tea wouldn't fix. Not that she had one handy.

'How?'

'I've called a taxi.' Croaky words, but audible none-theless. Maybe there were flaws in his chest musculature after all. She let her gaze drift downwards and swallowed hard.

Unlikely.

'How are you getting home?'

'The same,' she croaked.

'I can collect you from your workplace on a motor-bike, if you don't mind the ride.'

'I don't mind the ride.'

'Five-thirty suit?'

Jianne nodded again and gave him the address. Jake's teaching uniform involved loose black karate pants, the remarkably well-fitting T-shirt, and no black belt what-soever. His students were a ragged crew, mostly young men, and apart from their black trousers there was no uniformity there either. They wore any kind of T-shirt that pleased them or indeed none at all. No women, she noted. Not in this class at any rate.

'My advanced class,' he offered, noting her curiosity. 'Most of them have been coming here for years.'

They were all staring at her, every last one of them. 'Anyone would think they'd never seen a woman walk down those stairs before,' she said nervously.

'They haven't.'

'Oh.' Jianne reeled at the implication. Jacob was an extremely physical man. A man who enjoyed women. Surely he'd had women in his bed during these past twelve years? Even if he had been too discreet to telegraph the fact. 'So...what do you want me to do? About the pretending to be together. Do I kiss you good morning in front of them?'

'I wouldn't recommend it,' he muttered. 'Just smile and walk away, Jianne. I'll take care of the rest.' He took his own advice and headed back towards his students. Jianne made her way across the rear of the training hall towards the door, her shoes tapping out a rapid staccato that sounded wrong somehow, here within this gathering of warriors.

She turned when she reached the door. Turned to look her fill of the husband she'd run away from all those years ago. He looked her way, almost as if he'd felt her watching him, and she caught her breath at the intensity of that brilliant blue gaze. He was right about not needing a kiss, she thought with a catch in her breath. Because this was a vow—a reckless, untempered pledging of raw desire, dark needs and passion enough to incinerate them both.

Jianne raised her chin and held Jacob's gaze a great deal longer than she should have before finally making her exit.

At five twenty-five that afternoon, Jianne shut down her computer, leaned back in her office chair and stretched out the kinks. Her latest client was a Hong-Kong-based hotel group who'd just acquired hotel chains in Australia and New Zealand. They had in-house designers for all their Asian brand work but they'd called her in as a consultant when it came to their South Pacific acquisitions. Designing a new-yet-familiar look with so much background branding already in place sounded easy.

It wasn't.

The phone rang and she picked it up automatically. 'JB Graphics.'

'What does the B stand for?' asked Jacob.

'Bennett,' she said quietly, and there was silence after that, a silence that would not fill. 'I'm just finishing up,' she said awkwardly. 'Where are you?'

'Waiting out front of the building.'

'I'll see you there.' She hung up, and collected her shoulder bag and turned off the lights and shut the door. Minutes later she stepped out of the lift and headed for the massive glass doors that would take her outside and into the heat and bustle of the day.

This was the commercial heart of Singapore—orderly yet crowded. Expensive suits dominated the dress code. Elegant window displays added to the general air of affluence. The broad-shouldered angel-faced warrior waiting for her beside a mighty black road bike looked as out of place as she'd looked in his dojo this morning.

Not that Jake Bennett looked as if he cared.

He followed her progress through the crowd. Two helmets sat on the bike seat beside him. She stopped when she reached him. He didn't smile.

'I thought you'd be trading under your own family name,' he said finally.

'You thought wrong.' They stared at one another while Jianne fought the urge to lower her head beneath the weight of Jacob's fathomless gaze. 'My family have always helped me, of course. They give me access to office space and boardrooms, and a million miles of contacts. I don't go wanting. But I don't use their name.' She took a deep breath. 'My clients know me as Jianne Xang-Bennett. It's the name on my passport. The name on my driver's licence. Is that a problem for you?'

'No.' He ran his hand through his already untidy hair. 'I—no. No problem.' He shot her a searching glance. 'You're going to have to take your hair down to get the bike helmet on. Do you mind?'

'Is this a can't-miss metaphor to show—for the benefit of anyone who might be watching—that I'm a wild and wanton letting-my-hair-down kind of girl?'

'No, it's a safety requirement,' he said dryly, but his eyes warmed a fraction and that was all the encouragement Jianne needed. Reaching up, she started pulling out pins.

'Turn around,' said Jake, and moments later he was pulling out pins too. He knew where to find them; he'd taken her hair down often enough during their marriage. He'd taken intense pleasure in it. By the time Jianne's hair tumbled down her back her nerve ends were awash with sensation and visions of moments past were well and truly haunting her.

'You could tie it in a low knot,' he murmured huskily as he ran his hands beneath her hair and lifted it slightly before letting it fall. 'Or plait it.'

'And spoil the metaphor?' She turned and somehow his hands ended up on her bare upper arms and she ended up far closer to his big lean body than she'd anticipated. 'I don't think so.' She studied his face, seeing shades of the man he'd once been in the contours of it. A mouth made for smiling, though he seemed to smile so rarely now. Eyes given to lightening whenever he was amused and deepening to darkest sapphire when he was aroused. His fingertips were rough, the pads of his thumbs tracing slow circles over her bare shoulders.

Jacob knew his own strength and he wasn't using any of it and still he held her motionless beneath his touch.

Jianne moved forward a fraction as need coursed through her. Such a shameless pulsing need she had for more of this man. She lifted her hands to Jacob's chest—for balance, she told herself—and caught her breath when his lashes came down to cover his eyes.

'Is he here?' Jacob muttered huskily. 'Is he watching?'

'I don't know.' She didn't care. 'Maybe he is, maybe he's not. Either way we seem to have acquired an audience.' They always had; her and Jacob together. Perhaps because of the mixing of races. Perhaps because he was simply so damn beautiful. 'Should we play to it?'

'Oh, I think so. Audiences exist to keep a man civilised. Did you know that?' he murmured as his lips moved slowly closer to hers.

'I thought that's what leashes were for,' she murmured.

'Leashes break.'

'Even yours?'

'Especially mine,' he muttered. 'If you want to kiss me and make people think we're together again, now's the time.'

'Are you sure?'

'No, but do it anyway.'

Sometimes, it simply suited a woman to do as she was told.

The touch of a tongue, the remembrance of a taste once savoured and never forgotten. One stunningly erotic kiss to fill the need inside her. One steamy open-mouthed caress to make all those years of loneliness fade away. She wanted that from him.

She took it.

Jake thought he could control this. Here on the pavement in front of strangers Jake figured he could curtail his response to the woman who'd once held his heart. But he hadn't counted on Jianne's absolute surrender to the moment. The way she fed the passion that flared between them. Savoured it. Savoured *him*, with lips and with tongue and a single-mindedness that left no room for holding back. The deeper he fell, the hungrier he got and the more she gave, until finally he broke the kiss, and rested his forehead against hers, his heart thundering and his senses reeling from her taste.

He closed his eyes and kept them closed. Kept one of his senses firmly closed to her as he struggled to regain his mind and some small measure of control. 'Put your helmet on,' he whispered. 'We're leaving.'

She did as she was told, and he donned his own helmet and got on the bike and waited for her to settle in behind him. She found the passenger foot pegs easily enough. Her hands settled lightly at his hips.

'Ready?' he murmured as the engine purred to life beneath them, and when she said yes he pulled smoothly out into the traffic. He couldn't go home. Not yet, with the taste of her still coursing through his veins. The leash had held but only just, and Jianne's hands on his hips and her warmth at his back gave rise to needs too long ignored.

He wasn't a chaste man. He wasn't even a particularly honourable man. But initiating a sexual relationship with Jianne seemed wrong for all sorts of reasons and some of them even made sense. She'd broken his heart already, for one, and Jacob had no desire to repeat the experience. She'd asked for his protection and the *appearance* of a relationship, nothing more. And she hadn't even wanted to do that, he reminded himself grimly. She'd only come to him after Zhi Fu had forced her hand.

No, the *only* good thing to come of any of this was that Jianne Xang-Bennett trusted him to keep her safe.

From harm.

Jake gritted his teeth and gunned the bike beneath them. Surely, that much he could do.

There would be no bedding her. Extremely limited kissing. Maybe then he'd have a halfway decent shot at retaining his mind.

There was a homeware outlet coming up on their left. He geared down and rolled into a parking space on a whim. He couldn't risk taking Jianne home yet. His need to touch her was still too strong. He needed a distraction, any distraction, and the shopping he usually went out of his way to avoid suddenly seemed like the perfect cold-shower substitute.

'I need bowls,' he muttered as he shed his helmet and tried to ignore the feel of Jianne's legs folded behind his own, and the way she'd tucked in behind him on the seat. Rock hard and about to buy crockery. Maybe insanity had *already* taken hold.

He could feel his plan working as they stepped into the shop and entered the realm of rows and rows of kitchen items that ordinary people couldn't possibly need. A salesman approached tentatively as if unsure what to make of them. Jianne drew people towards her and always had, whereas he…didn't.

'May I help you?' the salesman asked.

'We need bowls,' said Jake. 'Plastic ones in a few different sizes.'

'You mean for mixing?' asked the salesman.

'He means for serving,' said Jianne.

'Oh. Table sets,' said the salesman. 'Western or Asian?'

Jake shrugged, care factor zero. Yes, this shopping business could kill passion stone dead. Something to remember.

'We'll look at both,' said Jianne, so the salesman walked them across two rows and down a ways before stopping again.

'We don't carry a lot of plastic ware,' he said. 'Most of our bowls are chinaware.'

'What do you have that doesn't break?' said Jake.

'Some of the chinaware is really quite robust,' said the man earnestly. 'Looks can be deceptive.'

'This one's nice,' said Jianne, picking up an oyster-coloured rice bowl so finely spun you could almost see through it.

'Ah,' said the salesman. 'Yes. Quite so, although not exactly what I had in mind for you.'

'Is it fragile?' asked Jake, picking up on the man's discomfort.

'Oh, yes.'

'Expensive?'

'Oh, yes,' said the salesman. 'Blame it on the Japanese.'

'I'm from Shanghai,' murmured Jianne. 'We often do.'

The salesman smiled suddenly. 'Think of the satisfaction you'll feel if you *do* happen to break one. You can blame it on all sorts of things. Japanese impracticality. Imperfect Japanese design. Inferior Japanese materials. The list goes on and *on*.'

'There is that,' said Jianne and turned to Jake, her eyes bright. 'I'll pay for them, of course, and naturally I'll replace all breakages—with plastic ones if you insist—but these bowls are really starting to speak to me.'

'Are they saying that if you buy them you'll be supporting the Japanese economy?' asked Jake.

'No. It's all quiet on that front.'

'Is this a female thing?'

'No,' she said airily. 'It's a Chinese thing. Grudge holding can be very therapeutic but it should *never* interfere with commerce.'

'Ri-i-ght,' he said dryly. 'Economic sanctions not really your thing, then?'

'Government-controlled commerce has a long and not altogether illustrious history in China. Makes us wary.' A faint smile crossed her lips. 'You want to talk global economic rationalism with me, Jacob Bennett?'

'Maybe later.' For some reason he was getting hard again. 'I came here for bowls and to make the memory of our kiss go away. I'm all for focusing on that at the moment.'

'Oh,' she said as her gaze rested briefly on his lips. 'Is it working?'

'Well, it *was*.'

'About the serving bowls,' said the salesman.

'We'll take them,' said Jake. 'Could you wrap them to go on the back of a motorbike?'

'But, yes. Bubble wrap's a wonderful thing,' said the salesman. 'Invented by the Americans, of course. Apparently they were trying to make wallpaper.'

'Really?' said Jianne.

'Oh, yes. Is there anything else I can interest you in? German cooking knives? Italian glassware? Irish linen? It's all here.'

'We're all shopped out,' said Jake.

'Are we?' said Jianne. 'I've never shopped for kitchen items before. Who knew it could be so therapeutic?'

'Put it this way. Think of the size of the kitchen you're buying things for, and *stop*,' said Jake.

'You're right,' she said on a sigh. 'You're absolutely right.' Jianne smiled winningly at the salesman. 'Is there a shop that sells bedroom furniture nearby? He has a *very* big bedroom.'

'Now you're hallucinating,' said Jake. 'We are *not* going shopping for bedroom accessories.'

'Coward,' she murmured. 'I'll be over by the pizza makers. They seem very manly and tough. Perfect for dojo living, in fact.'

'Enough with the purchases,' said Jake. 'Who knew that kissing you would be preferable to shopping with you?'

'Oh, I think most men could have called that one,' murmured the salesman. 'I'll wrap these over at the counter, shall I?'

'Wrap fast,' muttered Jake.

'Always do.'

Jake's bike lived in the storeroom just inside the double doored front entrance to the dojo. For ease of parking and practicality you couldn't go past it.

Jianne had a grin on her face and hopefully intact Noritake dinner bowls in the pack on her back as she stepped from the bike and pulled off her helmet. 'I'm quite liking dojo living,' she said. 'It's very streamlined. What *is* that smell?'

'Sweat,' said Jake.

Jianne's smile dimmed. Jake hid his. 'Po's around somewhere if you need a hand with anything. I have to referee a bout between two of my black belts in half an hour's time. It's an open house inter-dojo competition, which means we usually pull a few spectators. Should Zhi Fu come in while I'm refereeing he'll have access to you and I won't be able to prevent it. What I can do is arrange a minder for you. Someone I trust.'

'Do you really think that's necessary?'

'I don't know.' Fighting ghosts was never easy. 'Did you hear from him today?'

'No. Nothing.'

'Anything unusual happen at work?'

'No. Maybe he doesn't know where I am.'

'He will eventually, Jianne. And if he's as obsessed as Madeline says he is, and as dangerous as your uncle thinks he is, chances are he already does.'

'Maybe.' And maybe Jianne just didn't want to admit it yet. 'I'd like to watch the karate,' she said defiantly. 'What say you point out the people you trust and if I need them I'll make their acquaintance?'

Jake did exactly that on their way through to the kitchen and then took himself off, presumably to get changed out of his street clothes and into more formal dojo wear. Or maybe he simply preferred his own company to hers. Jianne unpacked the bowls, smirking somewhat over the bubble wrap and smiling even more as she set the beautiful bowls on the ancient laminated countertop. Maybe they *would* break in this rough and ready environment. And maybe they were tougher than they looked.

The evening progressed. A motley crowd gathered. Vicious fighting ensued and Jacob enforced the rules. Apparently there was a winner. Zhi Fu did not attend.

Later Jianne, Po and Jacob ate Chinese takeaway out of Noritake bone china bowls. Jacob washed up afterwards and Po cleared the table before silently slipping away. When the boy returned a minute or so later he earnestly presented her with half a dozen bars of pre-loved lavender soap.

Jianne thanked him gravely. She thought she heard a groan, over by the sink. She *definitely* heard the clatter of cutlery against Japan's finest crockery.

But the bowls did not break.

CHAPTER FIVE

JIANNE'S second night in Jacob's bed was no different from her first. Light filled, largely sleepless, and heavy on the erotic fantasies. Fortunately, she had a plan. It began with a blanket, a broomstick and Jacob's reading chair. The chair went beneath the windows that fed light directly onto the bed. Jianne stood on the chair, the blanket hooked over the broom. Up went the broomstick to push the blanket between the window panes. The closing of the slatted window panes kept it there. Getting the window panes to close on the blanket but not the broom was the trickiest part of the process but, frankly, she had all night.

The second part of her plan involved *A Comprehensive History of the Civilised World*—a hefty hardback tome borrowed from her uncle's research library. If the contents didn't put her to sleep she could always belt herself over the head with it.

The third part of her plan was only to be put into motion if all else failed. It involved creeping downstairs in a teeny-tiny singlet and fitted cotton boxers and appropriating a suitably large glass of Scotch from the bottle on the shelf above the kitchen sink.

She toyed with the idea of adding a large belted black raincoat to her stealth wear in order to cover her near nakedness but the raincoat was a little on the rustle-y side and would doubtless wake the dead.

No, what she really needed to do was buy a bottle of Scotch in her lunch break tomorrow and bring it upstairs when she came in from work, thus avoiding night-time trips to the kitchen altogether.

At ten-thirty a quiet knock sounded on her bedroom door and Jianne called out a wary 'who is it?' as she put her raincoat to use after all.

'Po,' said a youthful voice. 'I have some tea for you.'

She opened the door. So he did. Tea in a coffee mug that sat on a dinner plate. A strip of packaged sugar and a spoon completed the tableau.

'It's herbal,' said Po. 'We thought it might help you get to sleep, if you weren't already.'

'Oh. How very thoughtful.'

Po eyed her quizzically. 'Are you going out?'

'No, I'm for bed and for sleep.' Please let there be sleep tonight. 'Right after I drink my tea.'

Po handed the tea over, and then proceeded to eyeball the roof.

Jianne followed his gaze. Nothing up there but iron struts and warehouse roof. 'What are you looking for?' she asked finally. There were no rats—she'd have seen them last night. Probably not dark enough in here for them either.

'Water.'

'Ah.' She nodded wisely. 'I see. Well, thanks for the tea.'

'The sensei said to tell you there's a kickboxing class at six in the morning and that it's probably going to wake you but it finishes at seven. The one after that doesn't start until nine.'

'Tell the sensei that I appreciate the warning.'

'He wants to know if you need a lift to work between seven thirty and eight thirty.'

'Tell him I'll take a taxi.'

'Is there anything else you want me to tell him?' asked Po.

Jianne smiled angelically. 'Tell him his bed's very comfortable. Tell him goodnight and sweet dreams.' Because damn sure she'd be having some.

But instead, there was a great deal of tossing and turning and cursing of neon lights. There was fantasy, and imagination, and a deepening need for sexual satisfaction and for that she cursed Jacob.

She'd forgotten over the years just how deeply sexual their relationship had been. She'd failed to remember how thoroughly Jacob's nearness affected her, how all he had to do was look at her for her to want him. He'd looked at her plenty today. He'd touched her with his eyes and with his mouth and now she wanted more because it hadn't been enough.

Not nearly enough.

Would it be wrong to pleasure herself in Jacob's bed while thinking of him? Cursing him? Would she be able to look him in the eye tomorrow and not have him instantly know what she'd done?

Did she even *care* if he guessed what she'd been doing in his bed?

Come three a.m. and still wide awake, Jianne finally bowed to her body's demands.

Apparently she did not.

Jianne took Jacob's cue the following morning and came downstairs between karate classes, dressed for work in a modest skirt and lightweight top. Jacob nodded pleasantly enough as she entered the kitchen. He appreciated her not coming downstairs until she was fully dressed and ready to go each morning. It spoke of a consideration for his work and of not wanting to disrupt it and that was exactly what he wanted from her. Exactly how she *should* approach dojo living.

Only a madman would look at her all buttoned up for the day and curse her for not coming down those stairs a little less well put together. Only a man bent on self-torture would wish that she'd turn up for breakfast looking sleepy eyed and sated. Well pleased with whatever had transpired through the night.

He remembered that look about her. She'd worn it a lot in the early days of their marriage. The latter days too. Jianne might have been a fragile dynasty princess in so many of her ways but she'd also been the most sensual and uninhibited lover Jacob had ever known. A woman so attuned to his needs and darkest desires that no one else had ever come close to satisfying him the way she had.

Jacob watched through narrowed eyes as Jianne walked over to the counter and switched on the kettle. She reached up to the kitchen shelf for a sturdy coffee mug. He didn't have any delicate china teacups.

Yet.

She turned and smiled at him politely, every inch the poised and perfect house guest. No trouble, no trouble at all. Until something flickered in her eyes, something stolen and sensual and altogether familiar. If Jacob wasn't mistaken, here stood a woman who'd sought sexual satisfaction in the dark of the night. And found it.

What the *hell* had she been doing in his bed?

'Tea?' she asked politely, and when he sat back in his chair and glared at her she raised a delicate brow and smiled a sinner's smile before turning her back on him and reaching for the tea tin.

Jacob's opportunity for retaliation came fast on the heels of his rising ire and his rising libido. Jianne couldn't quite reach the tin that sat on the highest of the two kitchen shelves, not without climbing on the kitchen bench, which she was, it seemed, prepared to do. He eased to his feet, no hurry, no trouble, and when he got to her he boxed her in with his body and reached up for the tea tin. 'Sleep well?' he murmured.

'Not really. The neon lights outside are driving me insane.'

'Princess.'

'Just because you can sleep in a room that's lit up like a carnival ride,' she muttered. 'Sadist.'

'Me?' That was rich, coming from her. *'Me?'* He leaned in close and put his lips to her ear. 'Hey, you're the one who's been up there doing the naughty all by yourself, princess. Did you think I wouldn't notice? Or that I wouldn't spend the rest of the day wondering exactly how you helped yourself and where? To my way of thinking that makes *you* the sadist, not me.'

'Such a vivid imagination,' she murmured. 'Do you really think I would do such a thing? In your bed or your shower or maybe even in your reading chair?' She tut-tutted him next and pressed a stern forefinger to his lips in a gesture guaranteed to drive him insane. 'I have two words for you, sensei.' Two words and a world full of sensual challenge in her eyes. 'Prove it.'

If Po hadn't chosen to barrel through the door Jake didn't know what he would have done. There would have been kissing, of a surety. His hand in her pants had seemed an entirely reasonable method of proving heaven only knew what.

As it was, Ji took one look at Po, shot a panicked glance in Jake's direction and turned her attention to the making of tea. The rest of breakfast went by in a flurry of tea making and congee eating on Jianne and Po's part and silent seething on his as he tried to bring his rampant arousal under control.

Fifteen minutes later, Po was on dish duty, and he and Jianne were crossing the training-room floor. Jianne on her way to work, and Jake on his way to make sure she made it into the goddamn taxi without mishap.

'I can't believe you ever thought that living here with me—even temporarily—was going to work,' he muttered darkly.

'Hey, you were the one who agreed to it.'

'I must have been out of my mind.' That or he soon would be. 'You do realise that if Zhi Fu doesn't strangle you, I will.'

'No, you won't,' she said with far more certainty than was good for her. A slimly built man wearing a navy suit had entered the dojo and was making his way towards them. 'Customer?'

'Could be.' But it didn't seem likely.

'My name's Richard Low,' said the man without pre-amble, once he reached them. 'I'm looking for Mr Jacob Bennett.'

'You've found him,' said Jake.

Richard Low wrinkled his nose as if assaulted by a particularly nasty odour. 'Mr Bennett, may I confirm that you're the sole owner of this building?'

'I am.'

'Mr Bennett, it seems you have a few problems when it comes to compliance with building regulations.'

'Like what?'

Richard Low smiled pleasantly. 'Inadequate fire-safety measures in place, exposed electrical wiring, a possible breach of structural ceiling-beam requirements. Also non-compliant signage, and I notice you don't have a ramp for wheelchair access.'

'Karate being such a popular sport with people in wheelchairs,' murmured Jianne.

'Mr Low, is it?' asked Jake politely. The man nodded, 'May I see some identification?' Low's eyes narrowed ominously, but he produced ID within plastic that proclaimed him a building inspector. Jake kept hold of it. 'And the paperwork to accompany these alleged breaches? May I see that as well?'

'There isn't any. Yet.'

'I see.' Jake took another glance at the ID card. 'Mr Low, if you wouldn't mind waiting here for a moment I'll see my wife on her way to work, come back and verify your details with the proper authorities, and then accompany you on your inspection. You know how it is. Can't be too careful.'

Richard Low didn't like being sidelined. Ah, well.

'You've made a friend,' said Jianne as he escorted her towards the door. Jake sent her a speaking glance.

'Building inspectors drop by often, then?'

'Not in my experience,' he said. 'This unwanted suitor of yours. What does he do?'

'He builds roads. You think he has something to do with this?'

'Maybe. Or it could be someone else bent on making trouble. Maybe someone connected to Po. Could be nothing.'

Jianne looked conflicted.

'Hey,' he said more gently. 'If something needs fixing I'll fix it or I'll get it fixed. It's really not a big deal.'

'Please be careful, Jacob.'

'Concern for me? And here I thought you were trying to drive me insane.'

'Only a little.'

'Yeah, well, it's working.' He saw her into the waiting taxi. 'I'll pick you up at five thirty.'

Half a minute later he was back in his office and picking up the phone. Five minutes after that Jake smiled a tiger's smile at a sweating Richard Low. 'So,' he said. 'Where do you want to start?'

Five-thirty came around fast for Jianne. Jacob phoned through to say he was downstairs. Jianne took her hair down in the lift to save time and avoid the agony and ecstasy of Jacob's touch. He smiled wryly and handed her a helmet. His kiss came moments later, brief and unexpected.

'Your cousins dropped off a few bags of stuff for you today,' he murmured. 'Dare I ask what was in them?'

'Clothes, I hope. Most of my belongings are still in Shanghai, waiting to be shipped. Can we stop by a fabric store on the way home today?'

'What for?'

'Therapy, discourse, and curtain material?'

'If this is for the bedroom, I got someone in to measure the windows for blinds this morning,' he said. 'They'll be ready to fit in two days' time. We've rigged up some more makeshift curtains for you until then.'

Jianne stared at him in growing discomfort. 'You ordered window dressings for me?'

'Not exactly. I've been thinking about doing something about the light up there for a while now. Ever since the new neon sign went up across the road.'

The point being that thinking wasn't doing, and until she'd complained he hadn't bothered to do anything about it. 'Jacob—' How to put this without offending his pride. 'Would it be possible for me to assist with the purchase of these blinds? Seeing as I'm reaping the benefit?'

'No.' His expression hardened. 'When Zhi Fu comes to his senses, you'll be gone and the blinds will stay and then I'll be the one reaping the benefit. I live the way I live because I want to, Jianne. Not because I can't afford better. I can pay for blinds.'

'Okay.' Clearly there'd been *no* way to make that offer without offending his pride. 'I like the way you live, Jacob,' she said quietly. 'I think well of the man who chooses to live such a life.'

'It's not what you're used to.'

'Maybe not.' An old argument, this one, centred around Jacob's role as the provider for his siblings, and for his wife. He'd been furious when he'd found out how wealthy her family was. How wealthy *she* was. His pride had been hurt. His trust in her abused. His willingness to accept *her* wealth as *their* wealth had been non-existent.

'I know you think I find your world lacking, Jacob. I come in and start changing things and it seems like I'm criticising the way you live. I didn't mean to. I couldn't sleep, that was *all*. The lights from outside, they—'

'I know.'

'And I thought if I could just stop them from shining on the *bed*—'

'I know.'

'And I'm horrified that you've gone and ordered blinds you don't even *want* in some misguided attempt to make me feel more comfortable—'

'I want them,' he said.

'And now I've gone and made it worse by offering to pay for them, and now you think I'm throwing money in your face, when all I wanted to do was make my life easier without you having to wear the cost. It's like the housekeeper all over again.'

'Jianne, *stop*. Please.'

Jianne stopped.

'The room needed blinds. I've ordered them. I swear if it'll prevent another conversation like this one, you can pay for them.'

'Really?'

'Really,' he said gruffly. 'You need to sleep at night. And just for the record I should have said yes to a house-keeper and let you pay for one.'

'I should have told you how wealthy my family was before we got married,' she said in a very small voice. 'Just for the record.'

'We were young,' he said.

'Insecure,' she added.

'Out of our depth.'

'Completely.'

'It was chaos.'

'So it was, and you want to know something strange?' she said with a wry smile. 'It made me a better person. Not at the time. Afterwards. When I finally figured out what had gone wrong. Where *I'd* gone wrong.'

'I know the feeling,' he muttered.

'So, here we are,' she said. 'Better people. Capable of having a completely rational conversation about who's going to pay for the bedroom blinds.'

'Jianne?'

'Hmm?'

'It wasn't that rational.'

They ordered Indian takeaway for dinner that night. Tandoori chicken and roti, and raita and they ate in the tiny dojo kitchen, with the door wide open and the breeze coming in, the better to disperse the heat of a sultry day. The food was good and the noise from the streetscape outside provided a cheerful background murmur to offset the sporadic conversation of Jacob and of Po. Jianne didn't have a great deal to say so she listened instead as Po quizzed Jake on yesterday evening's karate match. The question being why the bigger student with the better technique had not been the victor.

'He's a good technician, one of my best,' Jacob told the boy after a moment's consideration. 'But he's never known hunger or homelessness, or fought for his life on the streets. Yesterday he faced a man who *had* known such things. Hunger and terror and viciousness and blood. That's why our good technician lost.'

'Have you known those things too?' asked Po. 'Is that why you win?'

'I haven't known any of those things,' said Jake. 'Not one. But I know the agony that comes of loss and I've lived in fear of not being able to protect the people in my care. I've known rage so deep that it threatened to consume me. I still have all of those things buried inside me, threatening to get out. When I fight, some of it *does* leak out. That's why I win.'

'I've known everything,' said Po with a bleakness that tugged at Jianne's heart. The boy wasn't grandstanding and he certainly hadn't made his declaration with any degree of pride.

'Then I expect you have the makings of a great fighter,' Jacob told Po, and buried in Jacob's words was a quiet acceptance of the boy, no matter what, no questions asked. 'Or a great human rights advocate if that's what you'd rather be.'

Po nodded, and the clumsy jerky motion quite unlike the boy's usual smooth movements told Jianne exactly how much Jacob's acceptance meant to him. Po from the dojo was quite a boy.

And Jacob Bennett was quite a man.

'Old man Chin wants me to help him in his restaurant tonight,' said Po, after a while. 'His nephew's sick so I said I would.'

Jacob nodded. 'Keep an eye out on your way home. Someone could be watching the dojo. They'll be looking to see what Jianne's doing here.'

Po nodded and a hard, patient look settled in his eyes. Shortly thereafter Po took his leave.

'What? No comments about a child Po's age being out on his own?' said Jacob.

'No.' Jianne took her bowl to the sink and, with her back to Jacob, said what was in her heart. 'What you said to him… The acceptance you showed him… The guidance and support… It was perfect.'

'He's a good kid,' said Jacob gruffly. 'And it didn't feel perfect. This kid…Po…his experiences are so far beyond anything I've ever known. I've got no idea what I'm doing. Whether I'm even helping.' He rubbed his hands over his face. 'God, I need a Scotch.'

She could do that for him. Put her knee to the counter to give her some height and haul down a glass and the Scotch bottle and pour generously as Jacob stood and came towards her. She could feel the heat in him. The tension, tightly coiled as he picked up the glass and drained it in one long swallow.

'Better?' she queried.

'Maybe.' He reached for the bottle. 'Want one?'

'Yes.'

He poured for her, and he wasn't being frugal. Same glass, which he held out towards her. 'You want a different glass, princess?'

She took the glass from him and downed the Scotch before handing it back to him with a cool smile. 'Yes.'

He got another glass from the shelf and half filled both this time, before handing her the fresh one. 'Better?'

'Thank you.'

'I told you I'd mended my ways,' he murmured. 'I have manners now. Of a sort.'

'You always did,' she countered. 'Of a sort. What happened with the building inspector this morning?'

'He's sending a report. Nothing to worry about.' Jake's gaze rested briefly on her lips. 'Not in the grand scheme of things, at any rate. In the grand scheme of things your unwanted admirer takes the hint and stops pursuing you, Po becomes a human rights lawyer, and I get my mind and my serenity back. It doesn't seem a lot to ask.' He stared down at her, his eyes darkening. 'Did you really do the naughty in my chair?'

Jianne took a great gulp of Scotch and swallowed hard before answering. 'No.'

'What about the shower?'

'It's a very nice shower, don't get me wrong,' she murmured huskily. 'But no.'

'I knew it,' he said. 'I *knew* my bed looked used and abused.'

'You are *not* getting a confession out of me on this issue, Jacob Bennett.' Jianne drained her glass and set it on the counter. 'Not ever.'

'More Scotch?' murmured Jacob silkily.

'Not even then.'

His smile came slow and lazy and shot straight through her. Jianne curled her fingers around the bench to either side of her and drew in a ragged breath.

'Did you think of me?' he whispered. 'Did you think of the things we used to do to each other as you pleasured yourself in my bed?'

Jianne shook her head emphatically to signal no.

Jacob smiled his tiger's smile as he moved closer and his body brushed hers. 'I think you did.'

Jianne closed her eyes. 'Prove it,' she whispered.

'Can't,' he whispered back, and his lips brushed the curve of her cheek before sliding down to settle at the edge of her mouth. He took her lower lip between his own and bit down none too gently. 'Do you ever think of me? Of the things we once did?'

'Do you?'

'Yes,' he murmured, and soothed with his tongue what he'd marked with his teeth. Jianne put her palm to his cheek, holding him in place as she slanted her lips across his and surrendered her mouth to his possession.

He kissed like a man who had known hunger and homelessness and aching, lasting loss. He kissed like a man who hadn't fed for years and was trying to take his time but couldn't.

Jianne didn't want him to.

Both hands to his face now as she feasted on the flavour of him, the sweetness and the savagery. Giving him every leeway to do what he would, take what he wanted and to hell with tomorrow. His hands on her hips, dragging her into his hardness. Her hands in his hair, at his neck, keeping him in place where her ravaging mouth could have him.

Gasping as he stroked long fingers down the crease of her buttocks with a sensuality that was his alone, down and down and then lifting her effortlessly so that she sat on the bench. His hands on her thighs now, pushing her skirt up and parting her legs wide as he stepped in close and dragged her against him again, and all the time his lips not leaving hers for more than a moment.

'I thought of you,' she confessed. 'I thought of you, and I made do,' she whispered as she slid her hand to his wrist and forced it down between their straining bodies.

'Like this.' And she surged against his hand as he took his cue and stroked her, his stroke so much bolder than her own and vastly more effective. 'Jacob?'

'What?' he asked hoarsely.

'I'm tired of making do.'

He moved fast when he wanted to, did Jacob, but so could Jianne. His belt went, the zipper of his trousers. He'd barely managed to drop his trousers an inch or two before she wrapped her arms around his neck and her legs around his waist and found her way home.

He broke their kiss with a gasp, and stilled as if he didn't quite believe they were doing this, but they were. He filled her and then some, and she had no intention of letting him go. They stared at one another for long moments before she locked her ankles around him for purchase and dug her hands into his shoulders and started to ride.

Jacob's sapphire-blue eyes fluttered closed as he picked up her rhythm with unspeakable grace. His lips parted and he sought her mouth again. Her gasps and his; wordless noises drenched in desire.

How they ended up with Jacob's back to the doorframe she didn't know. Or her back to the stairwell wall. Or with Jacob beneath her on the stairs themselves, with his shirt off and his hands fisted in her hair as she moved above him, every stroke a languid promise, every promise pushing her higher.

'Not yet,' he whispered as she leaned down into a kiss filled with a need so pure and perfect that Jianne gasped at its beauty.

'Too late.' Too late for her, as the undulating dance and the fullness of his possession ripped her effortlessly into ecstasy.

Jake ate her cries of completion straight from her mouth and they fed him as nothing else had ever fed him. Not for twelve long years. He made it to his knees, to his feet, with Jianne locked in his arms and with him still buried deep inside her. He made it to the top of the stairs before taking her down to the floor with him again, saving her the bruises by keeping her above him.

He wanted her hands on his chest and she willingly complied, her nails scraping tracks across his skin as he sucked in a breath and rode pleasure to the point of pain. Her mouth soon followed, her tongue laving his nipple before she bit down ungently. Impossible not to bury his hands in her hair and bring her head up and take her mouth with a ferocity she knew damn well he had in him.

No hiding from this woman exactly what he was and how he hungered. He couldn't do it—he'd never been able to hide his savagery from Jianne the way he hid it from others. She drew it from him effortlessly, fed it with every move she made.

Her nails leaving crescent moons on his forearms now as she took more of him, all of him and whimpered in the taking, her knees high and her heels digging into the floor. Easy to position her for unfettered penetration so that she rubbed against his shaft with every stroke, so easy to slake his thirst for more. Because she was just as wild in their lovemaking as he was, that was the key to it.

'Come with me,' he ordered raggedly.

'Make me.'

He never had been one to ignore a challenge.

He made her scream before he was through with her. He rolled her onto her back and made her writhe and bite and beg. He made her come. And this time he fell into oblivion with her.

Jianne never quite figured out how they made it to the bed. She remembered the top of the stairs, the madness of pure passion, and the ecstasy of surrender. She remembered feeling boneless in the aftermath and being picked up in strong arms and she remembered a kiss so raw and worshipping that her eyes had filled with tears and she'd had to close them lest he see.

She didn't talk for fear of breaking the spell that had brought them to this. She didn't say a word as he gathered her close, just pressed a trembling kiss to the bite mark on his chest, and tried to smooth away the ridges made by her nails.

'Don't,' he whispered and in his voice was an apology so profound she felt her heart tremble beneath the weight of it. 'I wanted you to mark me. You know I did.'

'I needed no encouragement, Jacob,' she whispered. 'I never have.' Didn't mean she couldn't tend to him afterwards. She pressed gentle lips to the welts on his chest, and wrapped her arms around him and held on tight when he shuddered hard and his arms came round her in a crushing embrace. Always so hell bent on staying in control was Jacob. Always so fragile after the rare occasions when he lost it. 'And I need you again.'

Slow and tender this time, to counter the madness that had overtaken them earlier. Wordless whispers and feather-light touches. Long, slow strokes as they took the time to cherish and temper that which had destroyed them before.

No words in the aftermath as Jacob held her, just held her, and stroked his fingertips over her skin until she slept.

CHAPTER SIX

WHEN Jianne woke it was as dark as it ever got in this room and Jacob was gone. Not over in the shower, not getting some clothes to put on, he was all the way gone.

The clock atop the bookshelf told her it was ten past three, which might go some way towards explaining his absence. Jianne's wakeful nights had caught up with her and when she'd finally fallen asleep she'd fallen hard. Po would have come home at some stage. Jacob would have gone downstairs to make sure of it. That was just his way.

But he hadn't returned.

Only the scent of him lingered on her skin and in his bed. No words of love as he'd left her, or even words that might make her feel more at ease. Maybe he'd been waiting for her to say them. Maybe he'd come back before dawn and hold her, just hold her, before starting his day. It was a slim hope but Jianne clung to it. At five-thirty, with the first faint sounds of stirring downstairs, Jianne gave up her optimism and headed for the shower.

Shortly past six, and with a karate class in full flow, she walked down the stairs and into the training hall. Her appearance was noted as she headed for the kitchen.

Students glanced sideways. Some of them stopped their exercises and stared. Perhaps because she'd washed her hair and hadn't taken the time to dry it completely and pin it up atop her head. She hoped it wasn't what she was wearing, because she thought it modest enough. A long-length skirt and boots and a modest camisole top. Whatever the reason for their stares, she wore their looks and returned them with cool composure.

One of Jake's younger students smiled and thumped his fist to his chest, heartbeat style. Jianne felt her lips tilt a bit at that. A moment later the sensei had him doing push-ups. Men hid smiles. Jianne didn't bother hiding hers. Jacob glared at her, Jianne lifted her chin and an eyebrow in silent enquiry before heading for the kitchen. Jacob was the one who'd insisted she sleep in his apartment and the stairs were the only way down. Let him berate her for it if he dared. Jianne wasn't inclined to make Jacob's life easy this morning.

Funny that.

Po was sitting at the kitchen table when she walked in, a half-eaten takeaway meal at his elbow and some sort of workbook in front of him. Simple schoolwork, Chinese characters that had to be traced over and then reproduced, she realised as she leaned in to look at it and pressed a kiss to the top of his head as she did so.

She didn't know which embarrassed Po most—her kiss or the fact that she'd caught him studying. He shut the book with a snap and blushed beet red. Jianne ignored his reaction and opened the fridge door instead.

Takeaway container, takeaway container, takeaway container, condensed milk for coffee. Water, beer, beer glasses, peanut butter, and eggs. The leftover butter chicken was tempting but, unlike Po and Jacob, Jianne did not do five or six hours of constant physical exercise a day.

Nocturnal activities notwithstanding.

An orange and a cup of tea, then, and a cup for Po as well. And maybe some thought given to grocery shopping, for in spite of her background of privilege and household staff Jianne knew how to cook. She hadn't always. When she'd married Jacob she'd barely been able to butter toast and hadn't really seen a reason why anyone would want to. Nowadays her cooking expertise spanned Chinese, Japanese, Thai, and French cuisine. She still wasn't overly fond of buttered toast.

'What time did you get in last night?' she asked the boy.

'Before one,' he said. 'I didn't see anyone watching the dojo.'

Jianne couldn't contemplate the kind of life Po must have led for him to speak so casually of working until one and keeping an eye out for people watching the dojo on his way home. She wanted to object to both activities. What she said was, 'Thanks for keeping an eye out.'

'Who's after you?' he asked curiously.

'A man. A very powerful and persistent man.'

'Did you steal from him?'

'No. Nothing quite so simple. He wants me for his consort.'

'Can you say it in Chinese?' he said.

'He wants me to be his companion, preferably his wife. Both our families are very powerful. A union would be advantageous.'

'Advantageous?'

'It'd be good for business,' she said, switching once more to English.

'But not for you,' he said solemnly.

'I don't love him. I don't even like him.' Jianne shook her head. 'A union between us wouldn't be very good for me at all.'

'So you ran away and ended up here,' said Po.

Jianne nodded. 'So how many words did you just learn meanings for?' she asked.

'Three.'

'What was the third?'

'Union.'

'Ah.'

'Sensei says I've got a good brain,' said Po. Not a boast. A trying-on of a new persona for size.

'I think he's right.'

'About what?' said Jacob from the doorway.

'Po's brain.' Jianne looked to the doorway in as casual a fashion as she could manage. 'Has your class finished already?'

'No, but I thought you might be leaving for work early. Po, you want to go out front and keep an eye on the class until I get back?'

Po nodded, and slipped away, leaving silence in his wake.

Jianne risked a more thorough perusal of the man she'd given herself over to last night. He had the faint outline of fingernail marks on his forearms. His T-shirt and trousers covered the other marks she'd put on him.

'I'm not sorry,' she said regally, and the faintest of smiles crossed his lips.

'I promised myself I wouldn't take advantage of you while you were under my protection,' he said in gruff reply.

'Noble of you,' she countered and sipped her tea. 'What was your position on *me* taking advantage of *you*?'

'I thought it unlikely.'

'Ah.' Jianne bestowed a smile upon him. 'No concrete position on that eventuality, then. Maybe you should come up with one and leave out the guilt.'

'Maybe I will.' He studied what he could see of her that wasn't hidden by the table. 'Did I hurt you?'

She had a bruise or two, in places. Was a little tender, in places. But the wildness of their encounter had been her choice just as much as his. 'I think I broke a nail,' she said demurely.

This time Jacob's smile went all the way to his eyes.

'Will you pick me up from work this afternoon?' she asked.

'Can you be ready to leave by five? I have to be back here for a class at about a quarter to six.'

'I can be ready by five.'

He nodded. 'We should go out later tonight. For a meal or a show. Somewhere high profile, where we'll be seen.'

'My uncle has a table reserved for a charity function this evening. That might suit. In fact, Zhi could well be there. Shall I secure us some seats?'

'Okay.'

'Okay.' They seemed to have run out of conversation. 'So I'll see you at five, then?'

He nodded.

'And I won't kiss you good morning.'

'Wise move,' he murmured.

'May I kiss you goodnight?'

'Depends,' he said as he headed for the door.

'On what?'

'Whether you want to sleep.'

Sleep was overrated, decided Jianne as she readied herself for the evening. People could exist on a lot less than seven or eight hours of slumber a night. People could quite conceivably exist on three.

For a while.

After a while a person's psyche got a little frail, their comprehension of events a little shaky. Take tonight's charity ball, for instance. It shouldn't really have taken this long to get ready for it. Her floor-length blood-red gown was a classic and a favourite and did not require ironing. Her hair had taken five minutes to redo and only required dressing with pearls to be complete. The application of make-up had been a problem seeing as Jacob had a shaving mirror the size of an orange and no other reflective surface in the dojo whatsoever. A harried call to Madeline, and ten minutes later Luke had arrived with a wall mirror under one arm, and what might well have been a car spotlight under the other.

'You're very kind,' she told him by way of thank you. 'May you have five children—all of them girls.'

'You don't scare me.' Luke grinned at her, completely unfazed. 'Maddy figured you might need a car for the evening as well. It's black, it purrs, it's parked in old man Chin's loading zone, and I'm really looking forward to seeing who out of you and Jake gets to drive it.'

'I don't have a Singapore driver's licence yet.'

'There's no justice in this world,' muttered Luke darkly. 'None.'

'Oh, I don't know,' said Jianne soothingly. 'Maybe your sixth child will be a son.'

Luke had left the room in search of his brother shortly after that and Jianne had turned to the application of a radiant complexion. Fifteen minutes later she was ready to go but for a decision on what jewellery to wear. Her grandmother's diamond and ruby choker for her throat, and matching earrings for her ears, but what about rings? More specifically, should she wear her engagement and wedding rings? They weren't showy—a small solitare diamond set in a wave of platinum, and a wedding ring that linked to it.

Jacob's wedding band had been of the same wavy pattern and twice as wide and he certainly didn't wear it nowadays. These days Jacob wore no jewellery whatsoever, not even a watch.

She closed her eyes, opened the door, and called down for Po. Within moments the boy was at her door. 'I need your help,' she said, and told him what she needed to know.

Dressing up in full black-tie regalia to attend a charity dinner with wealthy strangers wasn't Jacob's idea of a good night out. The thought that he might finally come face to face with Jianne's aggressive suitor helped sweeten the deal a little but, overall, his general mindset was not one of enthusiasm. His middle brother, the eternal optimist, wasn't exactly helping matters with his inside scoop on Jianne's aunt and uncle. Apparently Jianne's aunt was practically Shanghai royalty, Jianne's uncle held a similar status here in Singapore, and their marriage had been an arranged one that had gradually developed into a love match.

According to Madeline, when it came to influencing Singaporean society, Bruce and Elena Yi wielded only slightly less power than God.

So much for dining with mortals.

'Do I want to know the going rate for a seat at tonight's table?' Jake asked Luke.

'You really don't,' said Luke. 'Think of it as part of the Yi family's contribution to getting Zhi Fu off Ji's back and enjoy that ten-thousand-dollar steak.'

'You're not serious.'

'Aren't I?'

Jake swore, and started unbuttoning his white dress shirt. This one had button cuffs. For a ten-thousand-dollar steak he was going to have to do better than that. 'Where's Po?'

'Here,' said the boy from the doorway.

'Can you go up and get me the white shirt at the very end of my clothes cupboard?' he asked. 'On the shelf above it you'll find a shoebox full of old watches and stuff. You're looking for a pair of jade cufflinks set in platinum.' They'd been a present from Jianne on their wedding day. A Something New. She'd been trying to embrace western customs at the time. Heaven only knew how much they'd cost.

'Anything else?' said Po. 'From the box?'

'Like what?'

'A watch or something?'

'No watch.' He didn't have one good enough.

'Here, borrow mine,' said Luke. 'Best fake Cartier in the business, according to my good friend Po's very good friend Jimmy the Rat. The diamond chips are real zirconium.'

Jake took the watch and studied it a while. 'Nice,' he said mildly. 'How much?'

'Fifty Sing.'

'Po your go-between?'

Luke nodded.

'Deal done in Chinese, was it?'

'Most of it.' Luke shot Po a hard glance. 'Something I should know?'

Po shook his head.

Jake shook his. He'd sort it out later. Give Po the benefit of the doubt for now. Maybe the boy would come up with a reasonable explanation. Even a halfway reasonable one would do. 'You got a good deal.' Considering the very real possibility that the watch was the genuine article. The way this evening was shaping, Jake would probably come across the real owner of the watch tonight. That'd work well.

'Anything else?' said Po, looking a picture of innocence. 'From the box?'

'Just the cufflinks.'

'Because I could bring the whole box down,' said the boy. 'In case you saw something else you wanted from it.'

'Just the cufflinks. And the shirt.'

Po departed, swift as ever. The kid had speed and stealth enough to make even the most accomplished martial artist weep. When the power came—and it would—the boy would be a truly formidable opponent.

'What was that all about?' asked Luke.

'The watch or the box?'

'Not the watch,' said Luke. 'I'm not sure I want to know what's wrong with the watch.'

'Good call.'

'So what's with the box?' asked Luke.

'I really don't know.'

'Jake needs a different shirt and some cufflinks,' said Po as Jianne opened the door and ushered him into the room. 'He's not wearing a ring.'

'Thanks, Po.' Jianne tried not to let heaviness settle over her like a shroud. 'That's all I needed to know.'

Luke and Po had decided they would be Jake's chauffeurs for the evening and were waiting—along with Jake—in the training hall when finally Jianne deigned to descend the stairs.

'Oh, man,' muttered Luke reverently. 'You are so screwed.'

Jake took one look at his wife and felt every last bit of blood to his brain head south. 'Go and get the car,' he said.

'Po, you coming?' said Luke, but the boy stood transfixed. 'And another heart bites the dust,' muttered Luke. 'Jianne, you look amazing. Po and I are just going to fetch the car.'

'Thank you,' she said, and smiled.

Po beamed back. Jake closed his eyes and whispered a prayer.

'Yes, indeed,' murmured Luke. 'Completely and utterly—'

'Car,' said Jake, surprised he still possessed the power of speech. *'Now.'*

* * *

Jianne accepted Madeline's ride and the chauffeurs that went with it with unabashed pleasure. Motorbikes were fine modes of transport on occasion but this was not one of those occasions. Ball gowns preferred cars. End of story. Jacob sat beside her in the back seat, a heart-stopping example of masculine perfection. Not a comfortable companion—anything but—with his searing blue gaze and his air of barely restrained power. But comfortable or not he was the only man Jianne had ever wanted by her side—that much she did know.

The hotel doorman greeted them with alacrity as they stepped from the car. A lurking press photographer took a happy snap of them as they walked through the foyer and then whipped out a tiny handheld computer gadget and asked for their names. Jianne Xang-Bennett and Jacob Bennett clearly didn't ring any bells for the photographer but maybe something would come of it. Jianne didn't much care either way, except that the photograph defined them as a couple and that it might aid in her endeavour to get Zhi Fu to leave her alone. She never had been one to delight in the attentions of the press.

'How many people do you think you'll know here tonight?' murmured Jacob as a doorman took their tickets and they stepped into the glittering Raffles ballroom.

'Including you, my aunt and uncle, and my cousins?' she said lightly. 'Five. Five is an auspicious number. I'm feeling very hopeful.'

'Six if Zhi Fu's here,' said Jaccob and worry shot through Jianne. Jacob didn't look as if he aimed to make friends with anyone here tonight. He was all about quiet, lethal confrontation.

'You will be careful when we meet Zhi Fu, yes? He's not a man you want for an enemy.'

'It's too late for that, Jianne. He wants you. I have you. I really don't think we're going to be friends.'

'I know, but just don't…'

'Kill him?' suggested Jacob. 'Not a problem. This is a hospital fundraiser. It wouldn't be appropriate. Besides, I'm all about restraint.'

'You weren't last night,' she murmured and Jacob countered with a glare.

'Can we *not* talk about last night's restraint?' he muttered. 'Or lack of it?'

Jianne favoured him with a wicked little smile. 'Of course, if you *do* find your restraint slipping over the course of the evening, you'll let me know, right?'

'You really think you can contain me?'

'I'm pretty sure handcuffs would help,' she murmured.

'You'd have to get them on me first.'

'You don't think I could?'

He shot her a glittering glance just chock-full of dark promises. 'Well, you could *try*.'

'Maybe I won't use force,' she said. 'Maybe I'll use stealth. I could distract you.'

'You already do.' Jake looked around the room. 'Is Zhi Fu here?'

'I don't see him.' Not that she'd done much looking. 'Although I do see my aunt and one of my cousins way down the front. That must be our table.'

Jacob sighed. He hoped the steak was plentiful, because conversation was sure as hell likely to be awkward.

The conversation was not awkward.

Elena Yi was an accomplished social hostess, her sons were welcoming, and Bruce Yi was a man Jacob could probably come to like and respect. Quietly commanding, razor sharp, and the lynchpin of a billion-dollar business, Bruce Yi seemed to have no qualms whatsoever about linking the Yi family name to Jacob's. Plenty of power in such an endorsement. Plenty of responsibility when it came to living up to the faith the older man was placing in him.

Wealth and influence. Jake had never courted the first and he used the second sparingly. This wasn't his world. It was Jianne's world, and if there was common ground to be had here Jake sure as hell couldn't see it.

And then Jianne came up beside him and put her hand on Jake's sleeve and just for a second Jake *could* see how a man could put up with polite society on occasion if it meant keeping the woman he loved at his side.

'Jianne looks radiant this evening, does she not?' said Bruce, shooting his niece an affectionate smile. 'Your new living arrangements obviously suit you.'

Jianne smiled. 'Jacob's worried that I'm having to make do,' she said. 'And maybe he's right and it's not what I'm used to.' But dojo living had brought with it moments of unexpected joy and quiet pleasure and Jianne knew the value of those things. She knew how hard they could be to find. 'But I like it, nonetheless.'

'Liar,' murmured Jacob.

'No lie,' she said.

But Bruce Yi seemed distracted, and not by something pleasant. He stepped back to widen their circle, creating space between him and Jacob and absolutely no space beside Jianne. Moments later a tough-hewn man with impeccable grooming and eyes as hard as agates stepped into the breach.

Jianne kept her smile in place and her hand on Jake's arm. Not for a moment did she betray any fear. 'Zhi Fu,' she said quietly. 'Small world.'

'Yes, it is,' said the man, a smiling urbane serpent. 'I'm enjoying Singapore immensely. You?'

'Yes.'

'Jacob, this is Sun Zhi Fu. Shanghai industrialist, family acquaintance, and new neighbour,' said Jianne's uncle. Acquaintance, the older man had said. Not friend. Bruce Yi knew how to deliver a slight with impeccable courtesy. 'Sun Zhi Fu, meet Jacob Bennett, world champion karate master and teacher. Jacob owns a dojo here in Singapore. Of course, he's also my niece's husband, as I'm sure you know.'

Neither Jacob nor Zhi Fu extended their hand. 'I'm curious,' said Zhi Fu smoothly. 'What kind of husband leaves his wife to her own devices for a dozen years and yet refuses to let her go? Surely not a loving one?'

'Curious things, marriages,' said Jake, with a tiger's smile. 'Just when you think they're over, something comes along to tip the balance and all of a sudden they're not. Tell me, Mr Sun, do you plan to stay in Singapore long?'

'My plans are…fluid at the moment. It's a matter of responding to the situation at hand. As I'm sure you teach your students, Mr Bennett.' Zhi Fu's gaze flickered to Jianne. 'You haven't replied to my house-warming invitation.'

'I'm afraid we have other plans,' she said quietly.

'Some other time, then,' said Zhi Fu. 'For old times' sake.'

'No,' said Jianne, her fingers digging into Jake's jacket. 'I don't think that would work.'

Jake had played nice. He'd heard Jianne say no. It was time to add his not inconsiderable weight to that 'no'.

He looked down at Jianne and gently disengaged her hand from his sleeve in order to slide the back of *his* hand up and over Jianne's bare shoulder. She glanced at him, startled, and he sent her the hint of a smile, a smile just for her, as he settled his palm on the curve of her neck, with his fingers to one side of her neck and his thumb to the other in a gesture that was pure possession. Jianne's lips parted and her eyes grew slumberous and knowing. She knew this game, she knew it well. Tension, and passion, and a darkly sensual challenge. They'd played it last night for passion. They played it now for emphasis.

When Jacob finally deemed it time to look back at Sun Zhi Fu, the other man's eyes were flat with the most dangerous kind of fury. If Zhi Fu had been a martial arts opponent he'd be one that made seasoned fighters wary. There would be no mistakes. There would be no rules. And win or lose there would only ever be one man left standing. 'Goodbye, Mr Sun,' said Jake softly.

Zhi Fu smiled coldly. 'Oh, let's not be so final, Mr Bennett. Goodbye's not a word I like to use unless I'm speaking to the soon to be dead.'

'I'll keep that in mind,' said Jake.

Zhi Fu's gaze rested briefly on Jianne and whatever he saw in Jianne's eyes turned his lips thin and cruel. He said something to her in a dialect Jake didn't understand, and, with a curt nod for Bruce, Sun Zhi Fu was gone.

* * *

Jianne watched Zhi Fu's retreating back until she could no longer see it. His parting words hadn't been ones of acquiescence.

Jacob's thumb brushed the sensitive skin behind her ear in a gesture both reassuring and erotic. 'What did he say?' he asked, looking from her to Bruce as if either would be able to tell him, but Jacob didn't quite understand Zhi Fu's cunning, or that the dialect he'd used would have been lost on her uncle as well as on Jake.

'He asked me if I wanted you dead,' she said quietly, and the hand rubbing circles at her neck stilled. 'Jacob, I'm so sorry I got you into this. I know what Zhi's like. I know how obsessed he gets about…things. I know how fixed he's been on acquiring *me*. I *knew* I was putting you in an awkward position, I knew he was dangerous, and unpredictable, but I never *ever* thought he'd threaten your life. Please. You have to believe me.'

'Shh.' The thumb at her ear resumed its slow circles. 'It's all right, Ji. It's okay. He's trying to get you to walk away from me. He thinks you'll do it in some misguided attempt to keep me safe. And you're going to ignore him.'

'But—'

'Shh.' His lips were at her temple. 'I knew he might choose this path, even if you didn't. And I'm not complaining.'

Jianne whimpered. A public meltdown really wasn't her style, but reaction had begun to settle in and her legs had turned to jelly. 'I really need to sit down.'

'We can do that,' said Jacob gently, and moments later they were at the table and her uncle was pouring water into water glasses and table wine into wine glasses and handing them to her and Jacob.

Jacob smiled down at her, his eyes gently teasing. 'If you want my opinion, I think our meeting with your unwanted admirer went rather well. I didn't kill him. Always a bonus. And look on the bright side. Now that the battle lines are drawn we no longer have to attend his house party. Shall we send him a happy plant?'

'Are you completely insane?' muttered Jianne.

'A happy plant would be a most appropriate gift,' said her uncle and both men nodded sagely.

'And the death threat?' muttered Jianne. 'Is anyone besides me even *slightly* concerned about that?'

'He asked you if you wanted me dead, correct?'

Jianne nodded unhappily.

'Did you say yes?'

She didn't think Jake's question required an answer. A scathing glance would surely suffice.

'See?' he said with the beginnings of a smile. 'Nothing to worry about.'

'You *are* insane,' she said. 'Why do I always attract the insane ones?'

This time Jacob's smile came out in full. 'Do you really want me to answer that?'

Jake ate his steak and made sociable with a great deal more enjoyment than he'd thought possible. He phoned Luke towards the end of the evening and axed his brother's offer to collect them but accepted Luke's offer to keep Po overnight. He declined Bruce and Elena Yi's offer to drop them home as well, knowing full well that his tiny dojo kitchen wasn't up to the task of providing good coffee or anything else much by way of a nightcap and that even if he did do as politeness demanded and asked the Yis inside, there'd be nowhere for them to park their car anyway. A luxury taxi ride home would have to do.

Jianne didn't complain. After her initial outburst regarding Zhi Fu's threat she'd kept her thoughts very much to herself.

Coming back to the dojo was like stepping into another world. A world more squalid. Definitely more real—at least for Jacob. He looked around his cramped and ancient kitchen with new eyes tonight and then he looked back at Jianne standing in the doorway. The contrast didn't amuse him.

Whatever they'd done last night…What he'd set in motion by allowing her to stay with him…Nothing good would come of it. Nothing but new memories to replace the old and an ache that never eased.

He headed for the kitchen sink and pulled a glass down from the shelf. Scotch or water. Devil or saint. Which would it be tonight?

The water was closer.

'You should go up,' he said gruffly.

'Come with me.'

He braced his hands on the bench and drew a ragged breath before turning to face her. 'And then what? Do we go back to being married for real? The problems we faced before are still there, Jianne. Look around you. Take a really good look at what I have to offer.'

'I am,' she said, but her gaze didn't leave his face. 'And I do not feel deprived.'

She walked towards him, boxed him in. Watched his eyes darken before long lashes swept down to shade the expression in them. 'You know what I see? A man who put his life on the line for me tonight. A man who filled me to perfection last night. A man whose bed I would share again tonight if he was willing.' It wasn't cheating to put her fingers to his lips and trace the perfect shape of them until he closed his eyes, parted his lips, and his hand covered hers. She sucked in a breath as he bent his head and his tongue traced a delicate path across her palm until he came to her wrist. There he lingered, setting nerve ends aflame and her eyes fluttering closed.

She slid her hand into his hair to urge him closer. She wanted his kisses on her mouth but he set his cheek to hers instead.

'Tell me you want me,' he whispered raggedly.

'I want you.' She nudged his cheek with hers and tilted her head to capture his lips but he wouldn't give them.

'Tell me you like what I do to you.'

'You know I do.'

This time his mouth met hers willingly, his lips parted and his tongue gentle. Not the uncontrollable hunger that had driven them last night, this hunger went deeper and hit harder than that. Tonight wasn't about fighting what they felt for each other. It was about surrender.

His lips teasing hers as he bunched up the skirt of her dress and slid it up her legs. Jake sinking into a chair and dragging her down on top of him, his jacket and shirt gone and his belt buckle undone. The straps of her dress making way for his lips, his lips at her breasts and her hands in his hair as she offered herself up to him and the sensual surrender he demanded.

So easy to become lost in him, in the feelings he created.

Fragile panties ripping because they were a barrier he didn't want. Fragile folds parting to allow for a possession that filled her soul.

'Take your hair down,' he ordered. 'Take it down for me.'

She did as commanded, pearl-tipped pins dropping to the floor as his teeth grazed her breasts and his hips moved in time with hers, slow and undulating. She arched back, relying on the strength of Jacob's arms to keep her in place as her hair finally tumbled free.

Jake groaned and stilled inside her. Willing his beast back in its cage, willing himself to stay in control, just this once. Possession didn't always have to be about dominance, though that was the need that rode him hardest.

Sometimes it could be about giving in.

She slid off him then and took his hand and led him up the stairs and to his bed. They shed their clothes until they stood naked in the half-light and then she reached for him again.

'Would you do it?' she whispered as they sank down onto the bed and into a kiss. 'Would you let a woman cuff you? Restrain you?'

Only Jianne would ever have dared ask such a thing of him. Only for Jianne would Jake have made the decision he did. He never took didn't take his eyes off her as he lay back on the bed, raised his arms over his head and wrapped his hands around the wrought-iron bars of the bedpost. They'd stay there now, no matter what, until she drew them down. 'Only you.'

She started at his throat. By the time she got to his stomach he'd bent the bed bars but he did not let them go. He bucked beneath her hand as she slid down even lower. He died a thousand deaths when tip met tongue and tongue danced along his shaft. She knew how to touch him, to drive pleasure to the point of pain. She knew how to soothe him and destroy him all over again.

And still his hands did not leave the headboard, even when she mouthed him to the brink once more and then sank down onto him with a ragged little whimper.

He flung his head back and cried out. He strained against the words that bound him but he did not let go. Not until she slid her hands up his arms and past his wrists to prise his fingers from the bars did he rear up and fist his hands in her hair as the wildness inside him finally broke free.

CHAPTER SEVEN

JAKE woke slowly the following morning. Still in his bed with Jianne sprawled out beside him, lost to sleep. Small woman who took up a great deal of space, both in his bed and in his mind. As for his heart—it had always belonged to her and always would.

None of which made morning afters any easier.

The physicality of the sexual act was something Jake revelled in. Problem was, total abandon had always been followed by aching remorse and he'd never really figured out the why of it. Maybe it had something to do with him being too demanding when it came to sex—he who'd spent so much of his time trying to be the strong one, the calm one, the one too balanced to ever demand too much of anything. Maybe it had something to do with losing control the way he did and waking up and knowing he'd have to claw it all back and lock it down hard. Maybe it had something to do with his fear of breaking fragile things with the weight of his need. And maybe the why of it didn't matter one little bit.

All he knew was that in order to survive a night like the last one, a man kept his mouth shut and his morning fears to himself and tried hard not to reveal with excruciating clarity how truly dysfunctional he really was.

He slipped from the bed and padded around the wall to where his clothes had once hung. Jianne's wardrobe now, but there was a box full of old clothes in the corner and old clothes were as good as any other when it came to getting himself downstairs and into the dojo showers where he wouldn't wake Jianne with the noise.

He found a pair of old sweats and tugged them on. He didn't bother with a shirt. He closed his eyes and took a breath, wiling calm to come and take away his uncertainty, and fatigue to take away his need for still more of his beautiful and sensual wife.

He started across the vast expanse of space towards the door, his feet making no sound on the polished wooden floorboards. He risked a glance towards the bed. Jianne hadn't moved but her eyes were open and the desolation in their depths bit deep. He stopped. He ran a hand through his hair. 'Morning,' he muttered, and when she didn't reply, 'I have to—' He had to what exactly? Escape?

'Teach?' she murmured and propped her head in her hand.

'No. Not until nine. I, ah, shower,' he said next. 'Downstairs.'

'There's one here.'

True. This was true. 'I didn't want to wake you with the noise.'

'And you won't.' She eyed him gravely. 'But if it's distance you want, or need, go right ahead and shower downstairs. Or stay here if you like, and I'll get up and go in search of some breakfast.' Jianne glanced down and plucked at the bed sheets with nervous fingers. 'It's okay, Jacob. Go.'

It was her fragility that did it. Made him return to her, and sit on the bed and put his arms either side of her as he pressed a gentle kiss to her hair, the edge of her eyebrow, and finally her passion-crushed lips. He didn't know what she wanted from him this morning.

She was supposed to be under his protection. Instead he was devouring her every chance he got and dragging her down into a world light years removed from her own. 'I like what I do,' he murmured. 'I like the way I live. This is me,' he said raggedly as her hand came up to cup his cheek and her lips trembled beneath his. 'I can't be like those other men in that ballroom last night.'

'No one's asking you to be.'

'I can't give you the kind of life you're used to.'

'Am I complaining?' she whispered.

'You never do.' That was part of the problem. 'I never know what you *want* until it's too late.'

'I want some of your time of a morning. A look. A kiss. Acknowledgement of what passes between us in the night, even if it *is* so raw and needy that it's hard to examine it in the daylight.'

'You have it,' he murmured, and closed his eyes.

'Tell me you want me,' she whispered.

'I do want you.'

'Tell me you think of me when you leave me.'

'I always think of you.'

'Tell me you don't regret what happened last night.'

But that he could not do. 'I'll bring you some tea,' he said, and kissed her one last time before he fled. One last ravenous and needy taste of her and a desperate apology all rolled into one.

By Friday, the window blinds were up, Jacob had moved back into his bedroom and Jianne had not moved out. Jianne had put in a tentative request for the downstairs bedroom closest to the kitchen to be turned into a lounge room, of sorts. All he would need to do, she'd told him speculatively, was knock out the wall between kitchen and that first bedroom and she could take care of the rest.

A man was in big trouble when a woman started messing with his walls.

'How come, if she likes it here so much—and she says she does—how come she keeps wanting to change things?' Jake asked the soon-to-be married Luke and the ever-helpful Po as they stared at the wall they were about to destroy.

'The power's off, right?' said Luke.

'It's off. According to the building plans there's no wiring in this wall at all.'

'Brother, this is Asia,' muttered Luke with a curious lack of faith given that he'd already been all over the wall with a stud detector. 'Home of creative wiring.'

'No, this is Singapore,' countered Jake. 'Home of every building rule and regulation known to man. By the way, did you know that Maddy can get building alteration plans through council in a day? Tell her I'm impressed.'

'That's my girl,' said Luke, hefting his sledgehammer, showing Po how to heft his in the process. 'And if you ask me—which, may I remind you, you did—I think getting rid of this wall and opening up a bit of extra living space down here is a fine idea. Face it, brother. Your family's expanding. You have Po's needs to consider these days. The boy needs some growing space.'

'No, I don't,' said Po quickly. 'I don't even need a bedroom. I can sleep anywhere.'

And had, thought Jake grimly. But not any more.

'And then there's the dynasty princess to consider,' considered Luke blithely. 'You want her to stay, you'd better start considering her living needs. Besides, it's not as if she's asking for a miracle. She's asking for a couch.'

'I'm doing it, aren't I?' grated Jake and his brother shot him an angel's smile.

'Yes, you are.'

'So they're really going to do it,' said Madeline as she opened her apartment door to a waiting Jianne, and ushered her inside, before promptly walking Jianne through to the kitchen where Madeline proceeded to raid the fridge for nibbles. 'Knock out a wall, free up some living space, and hopefully throw in a new kitchen while they're at it. May wonders never cease.'

'I don't know what came over him,' said Jianne. 'It was only a suggestion. A throwaway one.'

'Also a good one,' said Madeline. 'Do we need to shop for furnishings? I think we do.'

'I can't,' said Jianne. 'When it comes to furnishing Jacob's home I'm feeling conflicted. I want to shop. I'd *love* to shop for downstairs furnishings. But it's not my place.'

'Even though you're his wife,' said Madeline. 'And you're living with him.'

'Estranged wife,' corrected Ji. 'And you're forgetting the reason I'm staying at the dojo in the first place. The murderous stalker.'

'Are you sleeping with him?'

'The murderous stalker?' said Jianne. 'Hardly.'

'Cunning misdirection will get you nowhere,' said Madeline smoothly. 'I'm taking that as a yes. Was it a one-of misdemeanour or is sharing Jacob's bed a nightly event?'

Jianne blushed and held her tongue.

'I'm thinking nightly,' said Madeline. 'This is, after all, a Bennett male we're talking about. Which means you're currently reunited and living with your husband as opposed to still estranged and just renting a room from him. Which means you do, in fact, have some say when it comes to household arrangements. As demonstrated by Jacob's willingness to tear down that wall on the strength of a throwaway comment.'

'Is there a point to this conversation?' said Jianne.

'Of course,' murmured Madeline. 'I'm thinking that if he's come this far already he's hardly going to object to a few new furnishings turning up. I'm thinking we're good to shop.'

Jianne chewed on her bottom lip. She didn't have Madeline's optimism.

'I'm sensing hesitation,' murmured Madeline. 'Is it a money thing?'

'Kind of,' said Jianne awkwardly. She wasn't used to sisterly confidences. She didn't really know how much to reveal. 'I have money.'

'Also a talent for understatement,' said Madeline dryly.

'Okay, so I have a lot of money,' Jianne amended with a wry smile. 'Jacob has considerably less money, although I wouldn't call him on the breadline by any means. It's just that we never quite figured out how to turn my money and his money into our money. He never let me use my money for anything and it wasn't just because of his pride.'

'No?' queried Madeline gently. 'Sounds like pride to me.'

'It's not pride,' said Jianne. 'You don't know him. You didn't see how hard he fought to give his brothers and sister a normal home life after their mother died and their father went…away.

'Jacob worked as a labourer and studied karate at night and he held that household together. He put food on the table and paid the bills and went to parent-teacher nights and made sure everyone got to play sport and be children. He gave up his time and his heart, and he laid down house rules and made sure that they stuck. Jacob provides for others. That's what he does, what he's always done. It's how he defines himself. It's why you sent him Po. Challenge that—try and provide for *him* for once—and you strip him, not just of his pride, but his identity as well.'

'Oh, sweetie,' said Madeline softly.

'I learned not to overstep Jacob's boundaries when it came to providing for his family the hard way. I don't want to go through that again.' Jianne looked away from Madeline's sympathetic gaze. 'On the other hand I am what I am, money and all, and if Jacob can't accept the things I *can* provide, and *want* to provide, then we don't have a future. Maybe we don't have one anyway,' she said quietly, and voiced aloud the notion that haunted her. 'Maybe I just want to hold onto what we *do* have for as long as I can and if that means pretending our money issues simply don't exist, then so be it.'

'Oh, sweetie,' said Madeline again. 'I'm hearing you. I am. But give the man some credit for growing up somewhat during these past twelve years. At least give him the *chance* to bend a little when you offer to provide. He might surprise you.'

'He did say he'd let me pay for the new blinds in the bedroom,' said Jianne. 'He hardly even flinched.'

'See?' said Madeline. 'I say we shop, and if you see something that's perfect for the dojo we just call Jacob up and see what he thinks. We're not talking about buying the man an island, Jianne. We're talking about buying him a couch. And possibly a lamp.'

'A sideboard would work in that space too,' said Jianne. 'Dark wood. Simple design. Useful.'

'You're absolutely right.'

Luke's phone rang just as the last section of wall came down. Luke downed his sledgehammer and reached for the phone that he'd left on the counter along with his wallet and a stack of keys. Jake stopped to wipe his face on his dusty sleeve, while Po leaned back against one of the remaining walls and grinned at the mess.

'It's Maddy,' said the boy.

'How do you know?' asked Jake.

'It's her ringtone.'

'Maddy and Ji are out kitchen shopping,' said Luke after he'd talked for a bit and listened for a while. 'Is there anything you want them to get?'

'Tongs,' said Jake.

Luke repeated the request and then sniggered into the phone at whatever was said in reply. 'That's not the kind of kitchen shopping they mean,' Luke informed them next.

'What other kind is there?'

'There's food shopping,' said Po. The kid was growing like a weed these days and training with an intensity the likes of which Jacob had rarely seen—little wonder he was all about the food.

'Apparently,' said Luke, not even trying to hide his grin as he held out the phone towards Jake, 'there's also the kind where you go out and you buy yourself a kitchen.'

CHAPTER EIGHT

'JIANNE, what are you doing?' said Jake into the phone with what he thought was a great deal of restraint.

'I'm not entirely sure,' she said. 'Although I am standing here staring at a kitchen that would be a perfect fit for the space you have available. Madeline seems to think I'm nesting. I tend to agree. The problem being that it's your nest and I really don't want to intrude.'

'Isn't it a little late for that?' he said dryly.

'Not really. I'm also considering buying an apartment. Then I could put all the things I've just bought in it. That could potentially solve a world of problems.'

'And Zhi Fu? Where does he fit into your apartment-buying plans?'

'Probably straight across the corridor. Which isn't a comforting thought. I may need to buy something freestanding, which is not easy here in Singapore. Also not cheap. Even for me.'

'Also not safe,' muttered Jake. 'Especially for you.'

'Exactly. Which is why Madeline suggested I call to see if you wanted a new kitchen, thus avoiding all other inappropriate purchases. They can have it installed in a day, and the surrounding walls painted, and floorboards sanded and polished as well.'

'In a day,' said Jake sceptically.

'One day,' said Jianne. 'As in tomorrow. Although you won't be able to walk on the floorboards until the following day, by which time the paint should also have dried.'

'Where *are* you?' he muttered.

'Renovator's heaven.'

'You really should leave there at once,' he said. 'It's messing with your brain.'

'And the kitchen?'

Jake closed his eyes and shook his head. 'Order the kitchen. Give me the shop's account details and I'll send through a deposit.'

'Jacob—' He could hear the hesitation in her voice. 'I'd very much like to pay for this kitchen, and downstairs living area refurbishment. As a gift to you and Po for welcoming me—however temporarily and possibly reluctantly—into your home.'

'How much?' he asked curtly. 'How much is all this going to cost?'

'I haven't gone mad,' she said carefully, although she *was* paying a hefty premium for the speed at which the kitchen would be installed. 'It's not some stainless-steel glory, and they're not furnishings no one would dare to use. They're in keeping with the dojo and the feel of the dojo. It'll be like bringing a little of what you've done with the space upstairs, downstairs. One of the couches is not even new.'

Couches? Plural? 'You're buying *antiques* now? For *here*? I thought you were in a kitchen shop?'

'We *are* in a kitchen shop,' she said soothingly. 'Now.'

'Tell her to get a wok burner,' said Luke. 'They're great.'

'Tell him of course there's a wok burner,' said Jianne. 'No Singapore kitchen should ever be without one. Is there anything else you want to add?'

'Yes,' muttered Jake grimly. 'There better be tongs.'

Two hours later Jianne walked through the dojo and tentatively made her way towards the kitchen. Her bravado while in the kitchen shop had been replaced by a growing anxiety that she *had* overstepped Jacob's boundaries and was about to find out by exactly how much. She walked through the doorway and stopped, eyes widening, as she surveyed the carnage.

They hadn't stopped at one bedroom wall, they'd taken out the next one as well. Enough space for a proper kitchen and a big dining setting and living space as well now. Beautiful space that Jianne knew exactly how to fill. If Jacob would let her.

Noise from further down the long corridor of guest bedrooms and a distinct lack of kitchen ware or food in the kitchen suggested that one of those bedrooms was currently being used for storage. 'Jacob?' she said.

'In here.' He appeared in the hallway, a dusty and dishevelled labourer, from the plaster in his hair right down to his steel-capped boots. 'Madeline not with you?' he asked silkily.

'No, she's due back at work for a bit. She just dropped me off.' Jacob headed towards her and Jianne's pulse tripled. 'Where's Po?'

'Luke's.'

'And your students?'

'Gone for the day.'

'This early?' His late class didn't usually finish until around seven. Jianne glanced at her watch. Seven fifty-nine. 'Oh.' So much for keeping track of time and returning home to a house full of people. She tried a tentative smile. 'I got you your tongs.'

'Really?' The darkly amused challenge in Jacob's eyes left her in no way reassured. 'What else did you get me?'

'Hardly anything,' she said. Apart from the kitchen and the couches. And the sideboard and a few other bits and pieces he probably didn't need to know about until they arrived. 'Much.'

'I've been thinking about your offer to pay for it all,' murmured Jacob. 'And my acceptance of that offer. I'm thinking that if you get to assert dominance in one area, I get to assert it in another. It's a balance thing.'

'Balance?' she echoed.

'Exactly.' He smiled a tiger's smile. 'And dominance.'

'You know, from where I'm standing you've pretty much got the dominance thing covered,' she offered. 'What with being the sensei, and Po's mentor, and my protector and all.'

'You forgot the sex,' he murmured, and took her shoulder bag and shopping bags from her. 'Right this minute I'm aiming for dominance in that area as well.'

'I'm really not sure it's possible to forget the sex, dominant or otherwise,' she offered soothingly. 'Believe me, I tried for twelve years. It can't be done.' But Jake had set his lips to her jaw and his fingers had found the curve of her spine, and Jianne closed her eyes and gave herself over to sensation and rising heat as she slid her hands beneath his shirt.

'Hands off,' he muttered, although she noted he was all about being hands *on*.

'About this revenge-sex plan because I dared to give you a gift I can well afford,' she said raggedly. 'You should probably know that I didn't just buy you tongs, I bought a whisk and wooden spoons as well.'

Jacob's teeth grazed her neck and Jianne arched into him and let out a gasp.

'Shower,' he murmured. 'Now.'

'You mean me?' She wasn't above making him work a little harder in order to secure her submission. Jacob thrived on a little hard work. 'Was that an order? Because, speaking delicately, I'm really not the one in need of a shower here.'

Next thing she was being hauled over Jacob's shoulder, caveman style, which wasn't exactly comfortable but did have the advantage of giving her a spectacular view of his beautifully muscled back and rear. 'You'll let me know if there's anything else you don't want me to buy for you, right?' she offered breathlessly as he headed for the stairs. 'Because I think I feel a shopping spree coming on.' She traced the curve of his buttocks with her hands. 'A really big one.'

'Hands off.'

Next minute a spray of water hit her square on the butt. Jianne squealed. Jacob laughed, and set her down, and dragged her beneath the spray, fully clothed the pair of them as he captured her lips with his.

'I was okay with the kitchen purchase, more or less,' he murmured as he shed his T-shirt and set to work on the zipper of her trousers. 'I was even okay with the tongs. But to buy a man a whisk and wooden spoons as well? Princess…' Jianne's trousers and panties went and so did her shirt and bra. Jacob's eyes darkened and his gaze fixed on her lips. His hands went to the fastenings of his own trousers and he smiled a sinner's smile. 'That's going to cost you.'

'Someone's watching the dojo,' said Po later that evening as he slipped in the kitchen door, via the back alley and probably any one of the dozens of secretive ways in and out of the back alley itself.

'Where from?' said Jake, shooting a lightning glance at Jianne. She had a tendency to get concerned about Po's nocturnal wanderings. Jake had a disturbing tendency to join her, though he was better at hiding it from the boy.

'The office block across the road and a couple of doors down. Second window from the right, five storeys up.'

'Could be just someone working late,' said Jake but the boy was already shaking his head.

'No.'

Almost a week had passed since their encounter with Zhi Fu at the fundraiser ball. A new kitchen had gone in. A couple of couches and a muted silk floor rug had gone down in the living area adjoining it. Jacob's nights with Jianne still ran to glazed and passion-filled torment. Sitting down to meals that she and Po had prepared filled him with quiet delight. He didn't want a house full of people all clamouring for his attention—been there, survived that—but this he could take. The order she brought to things. The quiet pleasure he took from it.

He'd thought he'd made a good life for himself here in Singapore. One that suited him remarkably well.

Well, now it was better.

Apart from a few niggly little things. An infatuated psychopath and Jianne's constant fear of what the man might do next being one of them.

'Blinds closed upstairs?' he asked Jianne, but she seemed not to hear him. 'Ji? You okay?'

'Yes.' She nodded and smiled but her eyes remained troubled. 'The blinds are open and so are the windows. It was hot up there this afternoon. I wanted to catch the breeze.'

'There was breeze?' he said with a lift of an eyebrow. There hadn't been any downstairs. It had been one of those still and humid days that frayed tempers and left a body lethargic. His students had been slick with sweat within five minutes of starting an exercise. Shirts had come off and showers had been plentiful. One of his regular clowns had put in a request for some more of that lavender soap.

'Well, no.' This time her smile was a little more genuine. 'What do we do?' she said next. 'About the watcher?'

'Depends what we want him to see.'

Po bedded down early that evening. The kid rarely slept for more than a couple of hours at a time—the kid was largely nocturnal—but that was residual of a life lived on the street and there was nothing either man or boy could do about it. Jake figured that Po planned to go walkabout tonight and see what a boy could see. He decided against sharing this suspicion with Jianne.

'Do you think it's Zhi Fu?' she asked in a subdued voice as they headed upstairs.

'Don't know.' Past caring. And when she went to press the switch that would close the blinds. 'Don't.'

She glanced at him, startled. Jake smiled back, an edge of pure cruelty riding him hard. 'If it is Zhi Fu watching us from that window, watching us now…What would you have him see?'

'That I'll never be his.'

There was a remote control to the new blinds over by the bed. Jake found it and when he turned around Jianne stood watching him uncertainly from over near the chair. He headed towards her and held it out. 'Take it,' he murmured.

She took it from him and when she did he trailed the back of his hand up her arm until he reached the strap of her pretty cotton top. He hooked his forefinger beneath the strap and began to drag it slowly down, moving around to stand behind her as he did so. Facing the windows now, both of them.

'No,' she whispered as he set his other hand to her hip and drew her back against his hardness. 'He'll see.'

'Then close the blinds.'

Jianne gave a soft strangled moan of protest and re-laxed back against him, tilting her head to allow his lips access to hers. He took it, open mouthed and famished and she responded with a sensual abandon that clawed at his control. She pressed the remote and dropped it on the chair. The blinds began to close. Over sixty metres of high slatted windows ran along that wall. The blinds did not close quickly.

Jianne turned towards him slowly, her hands going to the hem of his T-shirt, pushing it up over his head to drop unnoticed to the floor. She set her hands to his stomach and her lips to the column of his throat. Possessively, knowingly, and he fisted his hands in her hair to keep her there. The blinds had still not closed.

Just before they finally did, Jake rested his cheek on Jianne's temple and slid his hands to the zipper of her skirt and looked up at that fifth floor window across the way from them and delivered a message.

Mine.

The following day started normally. Jake took his early class as usual, and then breakfasted with Jianne and Po before seeing Jianne off to work in a taxi. He sent Po's schoolwork tutor through to the back when he arrived and he wrote up next week's training schedule on the board. Po and the tutor would write it out in Chinese on a different board.

By mid afternoon the weather was building towards a storm fest and only the most dedicated of students had bothered to show for his three o'clock class. Three regulars, including Po, and one drop-in. The drop-in signed in as Tup and gave a Thailand address. The name didn't register with Jake. The address did. Tup's town boasted fighting pits backed by syndicate crime. The kind of pits that made death by hanging look like a kindness.

Jake showed Tup through to the changing rooms and then drew Po aside. 'See if you can get hold of Luke,' he said. 'Tell him to get over here. Now.'

Po left and Jake set his remaining students to warming up and working their way through the forms. It took all of two minutes to decide that Tup hadn't come to martial arts late in his twenty-something life. Tup moved with the effortless grace of someone who'd been steeped in The Way since birth.

Jake knew his own worth as a teacher. He ran a clean dojo. He brought out the best in his students, and his world championship wins ensured that he commanded respect and that he *did* have knowledge to pass on. Knowledge that students didn't necessarily get elsewhere. Jake didn't often come across a student who surpassed him but he had *nothing* to teach his newest student that Tup didn't already know.

The man could have simply been in the area and decided to drop in to train—nothing wrong with that. But fighters of Tup's calibre didn't usually drop by unannounced, and nor did they give no details whatsoever of their experience.

Luke and Po arrived about ten minutes into the lesson. Po joined the class. Luke nodded and stood back, arms crossed, with one eye on the door, one on the class, and his back to the wall. Jake nodded grimly and kept right on teaching. Fifteen more minutes into the session they broke for water and sweat-stained T-shirts came off. The scars, burns, and welts on Tup's sculpted torso—some of them old and some of them not—told an ugly story and confirmed Jake's suspicions. Tup was a pit dog, and the fact that Tup was still alive was testament enough to his skills.

'We'll spar now,' he told a watchful Tup. 'Light contact one-on-one, no mats. You'll have your chance at everyone, including me. When your opponent hits the floor is when you stop. This is not an advanced class. You'll need to skill down.'

'What about the boy?' said Tup.

'He learns fast,' said Jake. 'And he'll learn from you. Don't break him.'

It took Tup less than a minute to down his first sparring partner. His second partner hit the ground in half that time. Tup fought hard, close, and with effortless grace and speed. Tup wasn't even trying. When Po lined up against him Tup studied the boy in silence and then showed him a purely defensive line to take against a close-contact body blow. Tup walked Po through the turn-and-deflect twice, showing the boy the correct centre of balance and the way the energy flowed. The third time Po lined up to repeat the exercise Tup stepped in close and without warning aimed an iron fist straight at Po's heart.

Po moved. Not gracefully, not quite the way he'd been shown, but he deflected the blow, whirled out of range of Tup's hands and feet, and lived.

'What do I do now?' said Po, and Tup's soulless black gaze swept the boy once more as if assessing his size, his strength and his potential.

'Where I come from,' said Tup, 'you run.'

'Bit like round here,' said Jake and stepped in front of Po. 'My turn.'

'I have a message for you,' said Tup.

'I thought you might.'

'I want you to know that I won't hurt the boy or your brother over there on my way out. You keep them out of this and so will I.'

'What's the message?' said Jake.

'Goodbye.'

And the dance began.

Lethal blows that came so hard and fast that to think about them before reacting to them would mean death. Pure instinct drove him, saved him, as Tup stripped martial arts down to its purest form and sharpened it with his intention. Intent to kill.

There was no rage. No hesitation on Tup's part as he continued his assault. Just a constant testing of Jake's defences, which held together, just. They wouldn't hold together for long. If he didn't attack soon, he'd lose. If he didn't commit to this fight completely he would die, might still die whether he committed himself or not.

Because another man wanted his wife and wouldn't take no for an answer.

Deep down inside—in the darkest corners of Jake's soul—a beast roared to life and broke free of its cage and with it came cunning and patience and stealth. And rage. Such a cold, controlled rage seeped into Jake and filled him completely—no room left at all for mercy or reason.

Luke said afterwards that the fighting had only continued for a few minutes after that. That he and Tup had both landed blows before Jake had crashed through his opponent's defences. Jake remembered taking Tup to the floor. He remembered his knee between Tup's shoulder blade and his arm around Tup's neck and he remembered that he knew how this next move went, the one that would end a man's life. He remembered Luke's pleading voice, and Po dragging at his wrists and yelling at him in rapid high-pitched Mandarin. He remembered Tup slumping to the floor as he finally let him go.

Not dead.

Nearly dead would have to do.

Jake had leaned down after that, with Luke holding fast to one of his arms and Po clutching the other. 'I'll patch you up,' he'd told Tup. 'I'll let you walk out of here. And you can tell the killer who sent you that I'm not going anywhere and neither's my wife.'

He'd kept his word.

He'd phoned Ji and told her to stay at work and not to go anywhere without her uncle or her cousins or preferably all three. He told Po not to go anywhere without Luke at his side.

Then he passed out.

CHAPTER NINE

WHEN Jake came to he was lying on a bed in one of the dojo's back bedrooms and a slim dark-haired man was pressing down on his pelvis. He shot upright and reached out to knock the man's hand away only to be blocked by another hand that had wrapped around his forearm.

'Easy,' murmured Luke. 'The doc's just checking you out.'

Jake eased back down gradually, due in no small thanks to the skull-splitting pain he seemed to have acquired. 'Where's Jianne?'

'Here.'

Jake winced, and it wasn't from pain. 'Why isn't she with her uncle or her cousins? Or Maddy?'

'She is.'

Jake had to think about that for a moment. His brain didn't seem to be functioning very well at all. 'So... they're all here?'

Luke nodded absently; his concentration was all for what the doctor was doing. 'They're christening the living room. Nice couch, by the way. Where'd you get it?'

'Ask Ji.' He tried to lift his hand to his head, started to raise his elbow, and groaned as pain threatened to overtake him.

'Dislocated shoulder,' said Luke. 'The doc put it back in while you were out.'

That would explain the nausea. 'Anything else I should know about?'

'Not so far,' said the doctor dryly. 'Fortunately, you still appear to have a functioning spleen.'

Luke hovered as the doctor continued checking Jake over. Eventually the doctor pronounced no lasting damage done, wrote out a prescription for some heavy-duty painkillers, and left.

Jake swung his feet over the side of the bed and elbowed up to a sitting position. No lasting damage done, no reason why he shouldn't be on his feet.

'A caring brother might suggest that you lay your sorry behind back down on the bed and stay there,' said Luke.

Jake just looked at him.

'Never mind,' said Luke, and, hooking an arm under Jake's good shoulder, helped him to his feet. By the time they reached the door Jake was swaying all by himself. Together they walked up the hallway and into the new kitchen and living area. Silence greeted him, bone deep and daunting. Jianne's relatives looked grim. Po had that hard, angry look about him that no child should ever wear. Jianne had her arms clasped tightly around her waist and looked to be on the verge of tears.

'Couldn't you have cleaned him up a little first?' Madeline asked Luke.

'I did,' muttered Luke. 'Can someone get this prescription filled?'

'I'll do it,' said Po.

'No,' rasped Jake. The free range kid would have to get used to staying a little closer to home for a while. 'Not you.'

One of Jianne's cousins took the script and headed out.

'C-can I get you anything,' said Jianne. 'A drink?'

'No.'

'I'm so sorry,' she whispered. 'This is all my fault.'

'No.' Shaking his head seemed like such a bad idea. 'It's not.'

He wanted her closer. He needed her touch, but here in this room full of people who watched his every move it didn't seem right to telegraph such need.

So he sat down at the table instead and he drank the foul concoction Madeline's housekeeper had sent over for him, and he suffered Madeline and Jianne making plans to feed everyone here at the dojo, and when Jianne's cousin came back and the pills kicked in he almost managed to relax. Bruce Yi went home. Madeline and Luke stayed on and so did Jianne's cousins. Apparently, they all intended to stay the night.

The idea that his row of shabby student bedrooms would tonight house an assortment of Singapore's finest made him laugh. 'Billionaire row,' he muttered to his brother, and laughed again.

'And no Scotch for you,' murmured Luke in reply.

He appreciated the show of support, the way they rallied around Jianne and carried on as if all were well and everything were normal, as normal as everything could be after a fight that had almost ended in death. This wasn't over—this thing with Zhi Fu—and everyone knew it. It was just getting started and plans would have to be made for increased protection for Jianne and for Po, and for himself.

Fighting ghosts again. A dangerous, unpredictable ghost who thought nothing of arranging the taking of a life or of pursuing a woman he wanted against her will. How did a man fight that? How did a man fight such intention without risking everything?

He thought he knew the answer but it wasn't one he liked.

But by nine that evening all Jacob wanted was a bed to collapse into. He'd have crawled off to the nearest downstairs cot hours ago but for the small matter of not being quite sure that he could stand up on his own. The idea of showing such weakness in front of these people disturbed him, but eventually Luke went off to lock down the front entrance doors for the night, and Jianne's cousins took themselves off to Jake's office to use the computer and make some calls. Jianne and Madeline were in the back rooms somewhere, making some last-minute changes to the sleeping arrangements.

He stared at Po. Po stared back in wary silence. What the hell kind of role model had he been for the boy today? Letting Po stand before Tup. Leaving him there when he *knew* there was risk and that Tup had an unknown agenda. If the kid hadn't had lightning-fast reflexes honed by his life on the streets he'd be dead.

'I'm sorry, Po,' he muttered finally. 'I failed you.'

'No,' said the boy, edging closer. 'You beat him.'

'He played me.' Jake got to his feet, using the back of the chair and the table for balance. 'I lost control.'

'Sometimes,' said the small boy with the fathomless black eyes, 'you have to.'

But a man didn't have to like it. Jake's eyes stung as he turned away and started for the door. He made it to the bottom of the stairs and thought that if he were alone he could slump down and sit a while, and crawl up those blasted stairs as the notion took him. Shoulder to the wall, he counted the damn things: twenty-eight in all. Maybe he could do it in stages.

He managed two before blackness threatened to engulf him.

And then a small and wiry arm wrapped around his waist and tried to take some of his weight. 'Sensei,' said a voice. 'Lean on me.'

'Thanks.' They managed two more steps before the stairs began to tilt alarmingly, but then a porcelain princess slipped in beneath his other arm and together she and Po kept him upright.

'Idiot,' she muttered.

'Thank you,' he said again, and together they made it up the stairs.

The blinds were closed tonight and there would be no opening them, thought Jianne grimly as she and Po deposited Jacob on the bed and with a troubled glance Po headed back downstairs. Jianne stayed, hovering uncertainly. Waiting for her cue from Jacob and wondering if—like Po—she shouldn't have just taken herself off and let him rest. Luke had told her a little of what had happened. That Zhi Fu had sent a fighter to the dojo and that he and Jake had fought and that Jake had won and the other man had left.

If Jake had beaten him and could hardly walk for having done so, Jianne *really* didn't want to think too hard about the health of his opponent.

'Can I get you anything?' she asked tentatively. Others had asked that question downstairs and the reply had never varied. No. Jacob Bennett didn't ask favours of anyone. Not even when he needed them.

'Can we try for a shower?' he said with a weary smile and surprised Jianne into silence. 'I'd like to get clean.'

So she helped him undress and she stripped down to her panties and a cotton singlet and she stayed within arm's length while Jacob got clean. She looked at the water sluicing down over his spectacular face and body and tallied every mark and bruise and there were a lot of them.

She'd seen bruises on Jacob's body before but nothing like this. So many of them this time, in all the wrong places. 'What did he want, this fighter?'

'Me,' said Jacob with his eyes closed and his face to the spray. 'Dead.'

Dread swept through her, a sick sinking feeling as she realised just how close Jacob had come to losing his life. Because of her. 'Luke said you let him go,' she said. 'If he came here to kill you why on earth did you let him *go*?'

'Because I'm not dead and I could never have proven his intent,' Jacob muttered.

'But you might have been able to prove his connection to Zhi Fu!'

'He was a professional assassin, Jianne. I don't think they do much talking.'

'So you just let him *go*? What if he comes back and tries to kill you again? And brings friends?'

'He won't.'

'Why won't he?'

'Because I let him live,' said Jacob, and the tremor in his voice cut at her soul. 'Be thankful Luke and Po were there and that they stopped me from ending him. I am.'

'I'm thankful for a lot of things,' she said as she stepped in and cut the water and gently began to pat his battered body down with a towel. He didn't protest, just stared at her with desolate, pain filled eyes. 'I'm sorry I brought my problems down on you. I'm so sorry for what this fight has cost you, body and soul. But I'm thankful for everything that makes you what you are. For your integrity, and your honour, and your strength that you so often put at other people's disposal. If Zhi Fu needs a reason as to why I could never love him, he need only look to you.'

'I almost killed a man today.'

And it was playing on his mind. 'But you didn't.'

'I wanted to. I was going to. I was crazy enough to.'

'But you didn't.'

'Because Luke and Po stopped me.'

'And who made sure that Luke and Po would be there in the first place?' she queried gently. 'Guarding your back. Keeping you safe, as you've kept them safe so many times before.'

He had no answer for that.

She got him dry and into bed, and his gaze didn't leave hers as she touched the bruises on his face with trembling fingers. 'I should let you get some rest.'

'Where will you be?' he said gruffly.

'In the chair for a while,' she said. 'Trying to read and watching you instead. Is that okay?'

'Yeah.'

She settled down and reached for a book. Any book would do. She tucked her legs up beneath her.

'Where will you sleep?' he asked.

'Next to you.'

'When?'

'Soon.' Just as soon as he'd fallen asleep. 'I want you to get comfortable first without me bumping all your bruises. Once you're asleep I can work in around you.'

'Ji?' He closed his eyes, shading them from her view. 'Can you come now?'

Not a declaration of love for he didn't love lightly, but a declaration of need from Jacob Bennett was wonder enough.

She took her hair down while he watched her through half-closed eyes and then she slid in beside him, half sitting, half lying, with one hand propping up her neck and the other resting lightly on his arm. 'Better?' she whispered and a smile touched his lips.

'Yes.'

She touched her lips to the bruise on his shoulder. 'How about now?'

'There's more.' His eyes had closed but the faintest of smiles remained.

'I know. I've seen them.' He had one high on his pectoral muscle. She kissed that one too and then she leaned over and kissed his mouth and then the bruise on his cheek, pushing her hair to one side so that it shadowed them like a curtain.

'Stay with me,' he whispered.

'I will.'

She stayed. And Jacob slept.

* * *

'For heaven's sake, will you please *stop* babysitting me?' Jake told his brother three days later. 'You're driving me insane!' The cousins had left but not before a state-of-the-art security system had been installed. Madeline had left after stocking the kitchen with food enough to withstand a lengthy siege. Luke had stayed to keep an eye on Po, and Jake appreciated his brother's help in that regard, he really did. But the way Luke and Po monitored his every move had a used-by date of yesterday and needed to stop. It needed to stop *now*. 'And should you be showing him that?' he asked Luke sceptically. 'Because I'm really not sure it's something Po needs to know.'

Luke and Po were in the process of *improving* the recently installed security system. From what Jake could see, this meant taking it apart, figuring out how it worked, and putting it back together only this time with booby traps for the unwary.

'Why not?' said Luke. 'I'm bored. He's bored. Might come in handy one day.'

'When? During Po's career as a master thief?'

'It'd definitely come in handy then,' said Luke. 'Except that Po's not going to be a master thief. He's going to be a martial arts expert and a lawyer. Aren't you, Po?'

'Yep,' said the boy, his attention not wavering from the tiny wire he was soldering into place for reasons known only to him and Luke.

Nice to see someone so focused.

'You know what you need?' said Luke. 'A little bit of relaxation and meditation.'

'Bite me.' What he *needed* was for Luke to get called out of the country on a job, the rest of his siblings to stop phoning him nightly, and for Jianne to stop treating him as if he were made of glass and might break at any moment. 'I'll be in the training hall.'

Luke looked up at him with narrowed eyes. 'The doctor said to lay off the training for at least three weeks. It's been three days.'

'Yeah, well, if I don't train I go mad.'

'Noted,' said Luke. 'But let me put it this way. If you do start training, I'm calling Ji, and she'll come home early and stare at you with that very weird mixture of adoration and guilt she's got going on and that will fry your brain even more.'

The kitchen door opened and Jianne stepped through it, grocery bag in one hand, laptop in the other.

'It wasn't me,' said Luke.

'Or me,' said Po quickly, sparing a brief smile for Jianne before turning his attention back to his nefarious-natured work.

'Don't look at me,' said Jianne. 'I just got here.' She set the shopping bag on the bench and the computer on the table. 'What's up?'

'He's bored,' said Luke. 'And he's driving us insane.'

'Oh, you poor things,' said Jianne with a kiss for the top of Po's head. The boy blushed. Luke winked at him and the boy blushed more.

'Maybe you could take him out somewhere,' suggested Luke. 'Get him out of here for a while.'

'But…is that wise?' Tiny worry lines had appeared on Jianne's brow and between her eyes as she stared at him with exactly the mixture of guilt and concerned *something* that Luke had mentioned earlier. 'I mean, what if Zhi Fu tries to have you killed? Again?'

'I'm sorry,' he said in as pleasant a voice as he could muster. 'I thought you came here to fight, not to hide.'

'He's a little testy today,' murmured Luke, shooting Jianne an apologetic glance.

'You think?' she replied, but her chin had come up and her eyes now held less worry and a lot more heat. Jake figured it for an improvement. 'All right, warrior,' she said coolly, in a princess voice that could have commanded an army. 'Where would you like to go?'

'How about a land far far away? I hear Tahiti's nice,' said Luke, and ducked his head to hide his grin when both Jake *and* Jianne stared him down. 'Just a suggestion.'

'How about a walk along the waterside?' said Jake. 'Maybe a meal somewhere afterwards.' Life as usual and to hell with Zhi Fu and his obsessions.

'Good choice,' said Luke. 'Instantly achievable.'

'When would you like to go?' asked Jianne steadily.

'Soon,' said Luke. 'Just a suggestion.'

'I can be ready soon,' said Jianne, and picked up her belongings and swept through the door without a backward glance.

This time, Luke wisely kept his mouth shut.

Jake wheeled the Ducati out into the dojo foyer while Jianne got ready to go. He ran a quick safety check, never mind that the bike had been under lock and key in the front storeroom since last he'd used it. Zhi Fu's fault for making him so wary and he cursed the man afresh for his obsession with Jianne and for making her so worried for the safety of the people around her.

She never said anything, of course. Or hadn't, until now.

But he'd wake through the night and she wouldn't be sleeping, she'd be sitting in his reading chair with her knees to her chest and her arms wrapped around her legs, watching him, watching over him with a fear in her eyes that cut into him like a blade. And then she'd smile and say she'd been reading, and he'd coax her back to bed and make her worries disappear.

For a while.

When Jianne came back downstairs, she was wearing a pale blue sundress. She'd taken her hair down from its bun and plaited it loosely down her back. Practical for when on the bike and just one more example of the concessions she needed to make when it came to dojo living and Jake's preferred mode of transport. He didn't mind cars and he wouldn't have minded owning one, but car storage was a problem here in Singapore and so too was parking. Want one or not, he had nowhere to keep a car so Jianne would just have to get used to taking her hair down and tying it back whenever they went out on the bike.

She hadn't complained so why the hell should it bother him?

It didn't. Wouldn't. No point obsessing over the things he couldn't give Jianne. The list was too long.

He handed her a helmet. 'You might want to hang on. We'll be heading out fast.' Zhi Fu's watcher was still in place, according to Po. They'd not get away without being seen, but he could make damn sure they weren't followed. Within moments of Po opening the dojo's entrance doors wide, they were half a block away and heading for the city centre.

When he was sure that no one had followed them he headed west to where the majority of the tourists weren't. To a part of the coast where the restaurants relied on the quality of their food and efficient friendly service to bring customers back.

By the time they'd arrived at one of his favourite seafood restaurants, fresh air and the burn on the bike had improved Jacob's mood considerably. By the time they'd been seated at a little table with cheap red candles and a paper tablecloth and their drink orders delivered and their food orders taken he was feeling positively relaxed. He liked living in Singapore—liked the access to different cultures it provided him, not just the vast array of food types to choose from, but the different atmospheres as well.

Jianne liked Singapore too; he could see it in her eyes and in her manner. She was comfortable here, even when they went downmarket she looked at ease. Comfortable in a way she'd never been in Sydney.

'Will you answer a question for me?' he asked quietly.

'Maybe.' Never the straight road with Jianne. Always the enigma.

'Why did you leave me?'

Not a question Jianne wanted to answer, he could see it in her eyes, in the way her hands went to her lap and stilled.

'It wasn't just our differences when it came to money, was it?' he said when it seemed as if she was going to remain silent for ever.

'No,' she said at last, her eyes guarded and sombre. 'It didn't help that I had money and wanted to use it and that you wouldn't accept it,' she said wryly. 'But it's not what finally drove me to leave.'

'Was it the culture shock?'

'Partly.' Jianne nodded. 'That was definitely part of it.' A sad little smile curved her rosebud lips. 'Nothing was familiar. I couldn't run a household. I couldn't recognise social cues. I couldn't *help* you the way I wanted to. The way I should have been able to.' She took a deep breath and let it out with a sigh. 'I didn't fit in. I failed you, and in doing so I became just one more responsibility you should never have had to bear. Even now with this business with Zhi—I'm still a burden to you. Still looking to you for guidance and protection. Some things just never change.' She looked down at the table and plucked at the chopsticks sitting there. 'At least this time I can function within the community. That's something, right?'

'Jianne, you're not a burden to me. And you're not a failure. Not then, and certainly not now. This mess with Zhi Fu—it's not a situation *anyone* could handle alone.'

'Thanks,' she murmured without looking up. 'But I shouldn't have dragged you into it.'

'Who else, if not me?' he said gently.

'That's the problem, isn't it?' she said raggedly and favoured him with a brief and rueful smile.

'Was it the family disapproval?' he said next. 'Was that why you left?'

'You've never really spent any time with my parents, have you?' she said. 'They're not bad people. They just… they've always had plans for me, you see. Marriage to a wealthy Shanghai boy and then a life spent in service to the family dynasty—*that* was the plan they had in mind for me. I doubt I'd have followed such a plan anyway, even without meeting you, but my family hadn't realised that yet. They looked at you and saw only rebellion.

They counted up all the things that didn't fit and called our marriage a mistake. They didn't see the love in it. Only the problems I'd taken on. They wanted me to leave you and when I wouldn't, they disowned me.'

'You never told me.'

'No.' She smiled sadly. 'I never did. I tried not to think about them but what I didn't realise was how isolated I would feel without my family behind me. How dependent on you I'd become for emotional support. It wasn't healthy. Jealousy fed on me whenever you turned your time and attention elsewhere. And there was always someone or something else.'

'You could have told me,' he said gruffly. 'I could have done more. Supported you more.'

'You were one man, Jacob. Hardly grown, with siblings to care for, dreams of a world title to pursue, and a wife who wanted more of you than you *ever* could have given. You want to know why I left you? It wasn't because I didn't love you. I left before I destroyed your relationship with your siblings and your chance at a world title just so I could have more of you for myself. I left because I wanted what was best for you and it wasn't me. I left because I wanted what was best for *me*, and I knew that if I stayed I'd come to despise myself. Any more questions?'

'No.' How did a man even begin to unravel all that? 'No more questions.'

She picked up her wine glass and drained it in one long swallow. Good idea. Excellent idea. Right up there with his newfound philosophy on letting go of the past and not asking any more stupid *stupid* questions about where they'd gone wrong.

'More wine?' he asked politely.

'Does oblivion follow?' she murmured.

'Only if you want it to,' he said. '*Or* we could try leaving the past where it belongs and sticking strictly to the present. I'm all for it.'

'Is this the present where I stormed into your calm and peaceful life, demanded that you protect me, house me, bed me, and now my unwanted suitor's trying to kill you?' she said.

'That's the one.' And he didn't have a lot to say about it that wouldn't touch on dark deeds and even darker needs. 'Although I'm thinking we should probably focus on the moment rather than the big-picture view. So... more wine?'

'Please.' He filled her glass and she set slender manicured fingers to its stem. 'Do you ever think about the future?' she asked quietly. 'About what you want from it?'

'Yeah,' he muttered. Nothing like staring death in the face to clarify what it was he wanted most from life. 'Lately I do.'

A note from Luke sat on the kitchen table when they returned to the dojo. Luke and Po would be staying overnight at Maddy's. The dojo was empty but for Jake and Jianne.

Jianne looked down at the note, dark eyed and sombre. Distant.

He couldn't have that.

'You know what I missed most about you?' he asked as he set his fingers beneath her chin and tilted her head until her gaze met his. Gentle because his aches and bruises demanded it. Gentle because his feelings for this remarkable woman demanded no less. 'The calmness you wrapped around me when we were together. It was as if we stood in the eye of the storm while all around us chaos reigned. My brothers and Hallie, they were a lot of work, more than a lot sometimes, and I know I didn't always get the balance right between what they needed and what you deserved. You always let us put our needs before yours, and you never complained, not once, and we never realised until it was too late how thoughtless we'd been.'

Jianne looked as if she'd rather be anywhere else right now than here with him but Jake wasn't finished yet and he did not release her gaze. 'I was their rock, you said, and maybe I was, but you were *my* rock, and things got a lot worse after you left. For all of us.' He took a deep breath. 'I'm sorry I neglected you. I wish things had worked out differently. Jianne, if there was one thing about your memory of our past that I could change it'd be your belief that you were a burden to me. That you weren't of any help to the family *you* were burdened with. You did help. More than you'll ever know.'

Jianne's eyes filled with tears. 'Can we just…have an early night and go to bed?'

'Separately?' he said and waited with his heart in his throat for her reply.

'No.' She buried her face in his chest and he held her, just held her, one frantic heartbeat to another. 'Together.'

'He has to go,' Jake told a half-listening Luke three days later.

'Who?' said Luke.

'Zhi Fu. I can't live like this. Forever wondering when he'll strike next. Jianne can't live like this—she won't stop worrying about *who* he'll strike next. Zhi Fu needs to go, then Jianne needs to go and then I need to go and get her back. That's the new plan.'

'Right,' said Luke slowly. 'Any chance of you explaining the latter part of your new plan in somewhat more detail?'

'I'd rather concentrate on the first part of the plan for now,' said Jake grimly. 'The part where Zhi Fu gives up on ever winning Jianne and goes back to Shanghai. Preferably without arranging my demise first.'

'People are working on it,' said Luke. 'Maddy says Bruce Yi's been busy. She says Zhi Fu's not finding Singapore's business world as welcoming of him as he thought it would be. He's losing face and he's losing money. The plan is that he'll eventually lose the will to stay.'

'I like everything about that plan except the time frame,' said Jake.

'It also doesn't address any murderous impulses Zhi Fu might possess,' added Luke, grim-faced and hard-eyed.

'The man can have as many murderous impulses as he likes.' Jake reached for the coffee tin and spooned some into a mug. 'As long as he doesn't act on them.'

'And how do we stop him from doing that?' said Luke.

'The hell if I know,' muttered Jake. 'I can't even stop *my* murderous impulses, let alone his.'

'That was self-defence,' said Luke. 'You didn't start it.'

'No, but if you and Po hadn't been there I'd have finished it. I don't think that's something to be proud

of, do you? I think it's something to fear. Inside me.'
Too much coffee, not enough exercise. The combination
was making him twitchy again.

'Everyone's capable of killing,' said Luke. 'First thing
you learn in the armed forces. It's the one thing you can
always count on. Up close and personal or at a distance
with the giving of an order; all anyone ever needs to
become a killer is the right motivation. People kill for
causes they believe in, or because it's kill or be killed,
or they kill to protect their loved ones. Those are the
motivations of the righteous. Then there's the killing for
fun or for profit. Not so righteous, those reasons. Then
there's killing for revenge, and motivation there can be
all sorts of grey. I've thought about this a lot.'

Jake stared at his brother, his coffee forgotten.

'More than a lot,' said Luke, looking uncommonly
wary, 'so if you want to discuss the moral ambiguities of
murder, massacre and war, I'm your man. What exactly
do you think I think about when I'm waiting to diffuse
a bomb or disarm a missile?'

'Living?' said Jake. 'Staying alive? The *job* you're
about to do? I'm thinking that might be a really good
approach to take.'

'All right, yes, I think about those things too. I go to
considerable lengths to stay alive—never doubt it. My
point is that most people go through life without ever
discovering exactly what it is they'd kill for. For you
that question came up and, like it or not, you got your
answer. You'd kill to stay alive and you'd kill to protect
the people you love, and if that gives you nightmares,
well, that's enlightenment for you. Always a two-faced
bastard.'

'Have you been meditating?' asked Jake.

'No. Why?'

'You sound so…wise. When did you get so wise? And how did you turn out so damn *balanced*?'

'I'll have to tell you about my oldest brother one day,' murmured Luke. 'The one who raised me and my brothers and sister. He's quite the hero. Loyal. Generous to a fault. Fiercely protective of the people he loves. Never *ever* walks away from a person in need, even when it costs him dearly. Doesn't always see the good in himself that others see so clearly—he's a bit thick in that regard. He's got this thing about always being in control and when he's not he cuts himself up over it.'

'Sounds like a basket case,' muttered Jake.

'No, just a man who holds himself to very high standards,' said Luke gruffly. 'Thing is, the most important lessons I ever learned I learned from him. Things like how to love. And when to fight.'

'I have to get Zhi Fu out of Jianne's life,' said Jake raggedly. 'Even if it means taking this confrontation places I don't want to go.'

'I know,' said Luke gently. 'I know.'

Men were not sensible rational beings, decided Jianne. Not when it came to protecting themselves, and definitely not when it came to Jacob realising that if he continued with the perfect husband routine for much longer, a woman might conceivably never want to leave.

They played at nesting for Zhi Fu's viewing pleasure, visiting household electrical stores in search of the perfect TV screen for the living room or desk lamp for Po. Sometimes they spent Jacob's money—for example, the TV. Sometimes they spent hers—namely the lamp, the bath towels, and the fifteen-hundred-threadcount sheets. The man had no idea of the sensory delight that came of lying on luxury sheets.

They played at nesting and while Jacob played his part to perfection, Jianne fell in love with the experience and had to keep reminding herself that none of it was real.

They hadn't renewed their wedding vows. Jacob hadn't declared undying—or any other kind of—love for her. They were united against a common enemy; that was all, and once that enemy had been vanquished Jacob fully expected her to take her leave. He'd even taken to pointing out particularly nice parts of Singapore where a single woman of good breeding and infinite funds might want to live. She appreciated his thoughtfulness, she really did. She made suitably enthusiastic noises and even checked out a couple of places with Madeline.

And then, under the cover of darkness and fifteen hundred threadcount sheets, she made him pay.

The problem was, the more entwined Jianne became in Jacob's life, the more at home she felt. The incandescent sensuality that came of being in Jacob's bed. The benefits of being part of a family unit steeped in more than one culture—benefits they passed on to Po, who added their experiences to his and flourished. She loved that Po turned to her now for assistance and advice almost as often as he turned to Jacob. She treasured that she was known around the neighbourhood now as Jacob's wife. The one—rumour had it—he'd kill for.

Or die for.

Something never very far from Jianne's mind.

They'd been playing happy families for almost two weeks since Jacob's encounter with Tup. She hadn't seen

Zhi Fu in that time, he hadn't phoned her, he hadn't sent her any gifts. The only thing he'd done was to send her a written invitation to lunch with him at one of the restaurants near her workplace. She'd refused the invitation—in writing—and had heard nothing since. She should have been relieved but instead her paranoia was growing by the day.

What if he turned his attentions to Jacob again?

Jacob was hosting a party at the dojo in three days' time. Not a regular activity for Jacob but one of his apprentices—the one before Po—had just finished filming his first martial arts blockbuster and was returning to the dojo for a few days of rest. When word had swept through the neighbourhood that Micah was on his way home, nothing less than a full-scale celebration would do.

When the weary Micah had heard, via Jacob, how many people wanted a piece of him, he and Jacob had put their heads together and decided to let everyone get their fill all at once, right at the start of Michah's stay, so that afterwards he might have a snowball's chance of finding the peace and serenity he was seeking, though Jacob doubted it.

Together, Jacob and Micah had turned a neighbourhood party into a movie preview, with a voluntary donation at the door on the night and the proceeds going towards helping displaced children acquire an education and a home.

Po had embraced the idea with fervour.

Jacob had embraced it with resignation, but he was no stranger to the power of the press or how to wield both his own reputation and Micah's to the charity's advantage. The party had grown as they'd invited more people to attend. People with deep pockets. Captains of industry and entertainment.

They'd invited Zhi Fu.

'He invited you to his house-warming,' said Jacob blithely. 'He invited you to lunch just the other day. The man's lonely. He needs to make some new friends and acquaintances in a safe and caring environment.'

Jianne sent Jacob a scathing glance.

Jacob countered with a cool and challenging smile of his own.

'What exactly is it that you plan to impress upon him?' asked Jianne.

'That your place is not at his side,' said Jacob calmly. 'And it's time he went home.'

CHAPTER TEN

'I DON'T like it,' said Jianne to Madeline over lunch the following day. 'Zhi Fu being so passive. Jacob getting caught up hosting this neighbourhood party and inviting half of Singapore along. What if someone slips up behind him in the dark and knifes him?'

'You really think Jacob's going to let that happen? Or Luke, for that matter? Or Po? Po'll have a knife-wielding stranger picked out and possibly picked over in seconds.'

Jianne closed her eyes and shook her head. 'You're right. You're absolutely right. So why am I still out of my mind with worry for them all?'

'Maybe it's because you've had more experience when it comes to dealing with Zhi Fu. Or maybe it's because you haven't quite come to terms yet with your love for a certain stern dojo sensei who'll do whatever it takes to protect you.'

'Believe me,' said Jianne grimly, 'I have had twelve years to come to terms with my love for that man. I'm good with it. More than a little familiar with it. What I'm not familiar with is fearing for his life.'

'It takes a little getting used to, I will admit,' said Madeline wryly, and Jianne remembered, belatedly, that in the course of his work Luke regularly put his life on the line and that if there was one person who knew all about this kind of worry for the safety of another it was Madeline.

'Madeline, I'm so sorry,' she said earnestly. 'I'm not usually quite so insensitive. I'm just—'

'Worried,' said Madeline. 'I know. I know exactly what it's like to have your imagination work overtime when it comes to imagining the worst.'

'How do you cope?' asked Jianne.

'One of the big tricks is to trust that they know what they're doing,' said Madeline. 'Zhi Fu's slippery, I know. And dangerous. But Jacob can be a *very* formidable opponent when he needs to be. When he's protecting the woman he loves, for example.'

'He never speaks of love,' said Jianne awkwardly.

'Do you?'

Jianne sat back and ran a hand through her hair. The hair she'd let fall freely today and to hell with her professional image. 'I was waiting.'

'For *what*?' said Madeline.

'For things to get a little less…complicated.'

'Good luck with that,' said Madeline dryly.

'You think I should tell him that I love him now?'

'I do,' said Madeline.

'As in today?'

Madeline nodded.

'When I get home this afternoon?'

Madeline nodded again, her amusement on the increase.

'After I've showered, and changed, and I'm looking my best?'

'Trust me, he's really not going to care what y⸻
look like,' murmured Madeline. 'But if it helps with the
confidence, by all means frock up.'

'I will,' said Jianne as butterflies began to whirl in
her stomach.

'Okay,' said Madeline.

Jacob took in his stride Jianne's mid-afternoon call
saying she was going dress shopping with Madeline
after work and that Madeline would drop her home.
He'd grown used to picking Jianne up from work, grown
accustomed to seeing the quiet pleasure in her eyes as
she walked across the crowded afternoon pavement towards him. Dress shopping, however, was something
he was perfectly willing to forgo in favour of sorting
out last-minute party details on the phone with Micah
and then working out his restlessness on his six p.m.
masterclass.

'I'm locking up out front and heading down to Chin's
to talk catering for this party,' Jake told Po come seven
o'clock. Jianne still wasn't home but she'd called to say
she and Madeline were at Luke's and that she wouldn't
be too much longer. Jake figured he might as well get
his meeting with Chin over with before she arrived.
'You want to come?'

Po looked down at the bulky Chinese dictionary in
front of him, and then at the messy columns of characters he'd written on a nearby sheet of paper. 'Can I
come in a bit?' he said. 'I wanted to get this done before
Jianne comes home.'

'What is it?' asked Jake.

'It's the words to a song, only I'm not sure about
some of the words,' said Po. Not an easy language to

learn to write, Chinese. Even when you were fluent in the speaking of it. 'Jianne's been helping me with it. She just *knows*.'

'I know.'

'And she can cook.'

'I noticed,' murmured Jake, wondering just where the kid was going with all this, but Po knew exactly how to say only so much and keep the bulk of his thoughts to himself. Maybe Po had been taking lessons on that from Jianne as well. 'Call me if you need me. Lock up if you go out. Jianne should be in soon anyway, and I'll be back in about half an hour.'

He was sorely tempted to add the words, 'and don't go anywhere without checking with me first' but to do that would be to let Zhi Fu dictate how they lived their lives and Jake was having none of that. He'd already turned the dojo into a fortress. Damned if he was going to give Zhi Fu the satisfaction of making Jianne and Po live as prisoners in it.

Po nodded, and Jake left and walked the two blocks down and one block over to Chin's Chinese restaurant. The old restaurateur was expecting him. Jake and old man Chin had a long and noble association based on takeaway food, a love of karate, and the occasional Friday morning game of Mah Jong.

'How many people?' said Chin as they sat in the corner booth of Chin's restaurant, the booth he reserved for business and the surveying of the busy streetscape outside.

'Say two hundred to two hundred and fifty, best guess.'

'Which one is it?' said Chin. 'Two hundred or two fifty?'

'I'm thinking three hundred should cover it,' said Jake.

'*Three* hundred now? Who's paying for all this?'

'The film studio, apparently. Something about it being a remarkable opportunity to showcase the humble yet suitably roughhouse reputation of their latest star.'

'Three hundred it is,' murmured Chin.

'And we'll need waiters,' said Jake. 'Waitwomen. Whatever. And drinks.'

'You want a *liquor* licence now?'

'Do I *need* a liquor licence for this?'

'For a private party, no. For what you and Micah have turned it into, I'm thinking yes.'

They were still debating the merits of various types of licensing arrangements when Po turned up.

'The master's apprentice appears,' said Chin. 'Best kitchen boy I ever had. You going to work for me in the kitchen on party night?'

But Jacob shook his head before Po could reply. 'He'll be too busy keeping an eye on the crowd for me.'

'Ah. Bouncer now, is it?' teased Chin and Po's smile came quick and warm.

'Jianne's home,' Po told Jake. 'She wants to know if you're bringing dinner home or if you want her to cook.'

'Tell her I'm bringing dinner home with me and that I won't be long.'

'Pretty woman, that wife of yours,' murmured Chin as Po took off home.

'I think so,' said Jake.

'You planning on keeping her this time around?'

'Depends,' said Jake.

'On what?'

'On whether she wants to stay.'

'Have you asked her to stay?' asked Chin.

'Not yet, but I will. Soon.' Just as soon as Zhi Fu was out of the picture and Jianne actually had a *choice* when it came to staying with him or not.

When the first sirens sounded, Jake and Chin looked up and watched as a fire truck went by. But the siren cut out fast and the focus returned to party catering plans. When the second truck screamed past and the siren kept on sounding and didn't fade away with distance, they went out onto the street to see what they could see. Lots of close-built high-rise buildings around this neighbourhood and fire in them wasn't pretty. Lots of back-alley restaurant kitchens too and sometimes they were hard to get water to.

Jake narrowed his eyes and stared down the street in the direction the fire truck had gone. Dusk had descended and neon had begun to glow, making smoke hard to see unless there was a lot of it.

There wasn't a lot of it, but there was enough.

'Looks like it's over near you,' said Chin. 'You want to finish this later?'

Jake nodded, eyes narrowed.

Chin nodded too as an ambulance sped by. 'Go. Send Po back for the food.'

Jake headed for the dojo, not at a run but not exactly at a dawdle either. By the time he reached the corner of his block, he was pushing his way through a crowd that had come to a standstill. His heart kicked hard as he saw where the fire trucks were positioned. It kicked harder still when he saw which building was on fire. His building, no one else's. Not yet at any rate, for the dojo was well and truly alight. Out of control alight.

Terror found him next. Found him and cruelled him as he began to run in earnest. Past the fire vehicles and the shouting firefighters connecting hoses to hydrants. Past other firefighters already wielding hoses, past them all until he drew level with the frontline firefighter who stood shooting water through the gaping maw that had once been the dojo's front entrance. There he stopped, eyes burning with every searing breath he took as he stared into the inferno beyond.

'Get back,' roared the firefighter.

'There's a woman living here,' he roared back. 'And a boy. Have you seen them?'

But the fireman shook his head and flame bellowed out the door and the searing heat pushed them both back. Not that way, then. No way in through that, or out. Side alley instead.

Every second felt like a slice of for ever as Jake ran towards the alley. But he couldn't even get close. The entire Eastern wall had gone up in flames and the firefighters there weren't even trying to stop it from burning. They'd turned their hoses to the walls of the buildings on the other side of the alleyway instead. Ash and water and fuel-hungry flame. Where were they? Where the hell were Jianne and Po?

The heat drove him back, always back, never forward. Po knew a dozen ways out of the back alley. So many different ways to get out and circle back around if they'd been able to make it out of the dojo at all. Surely if they'd been in the downstairs living area they'd have made it out the side door before the entire wall went up in flames? How the hell did a building burn so *fast*?

He looked up to the second floor again, and the place where windows and blinds had once been. Looked up to the room he shared with Jianne and saw only flames.

No.

Not there. She couldn't be up there. She couldn't be anywhere in there.

'Sir, you have to get *back*,' said a uniformed voice, an ambulance officer this time. 'We're asking everybody to stay back.'

'I live here,' he said. 'With my wife and my boy. Have you seen them?'

'No, sir. Maybe if you come over by the ambulance and wait…'

'There's a back alley,' he muttered. 'They could have gone out the back. Through shops and buildings on the next street over.' And then he was pushing his way back through the crowd, feet and heart pounding as he ploughed his way to the first corner and then along the street to the next. They'd begun to evacuate this street too, but the second building along—a restaurant—had a back entrance to the far end of the alley. Jake knew the owners and they let him pass through—no, they hadn't seen Po and they hadn't seen his wife.

Garbage skips and shadows, the alleyway was full of them. Full of firefighters too, for they'd come through the shops further up, dragging hoses behind them in their quest to contain the blaze. The flames weren't as bad this side of the dojo. The back bedrooms still stood. Naked flame didn't suck every last bit of oxygen from the air. *'Jianne,'* he roared. *'Po.'*

And something moved on a rooftop, halfway down the alley. A silhouette, and then a voice. 'Sensei, up here.'

Jake groaned, only it was more of a sob as his legs threatened to give way beneath him and he sagged against the wall for support. 'Both of you?'

'Just me.'

'Where's Jianne?' he said in a voice that threatened to crack.

'I don't know.'

And the horror began all over again.

'I came home the back way,' Po called down. 'And the dojo was on fire but not as much as now. I went in through the bedrooms and made it to the kitchen but I couldn't get into the training hall or up the stairs. She wasn't in the kitchen. She was in the kitchen when I left.'

Jake put his hands to his knees and stared at the ground. Smoke stung his eyes. Made them water. 'You shouldn't have gone in there. What the hell were you *thinking*?'

'You would have.'

Jake took a deep breath and ran a hand through his hair.

'I can see inside the upstairs windows from here,' said Po next. 'Jianne would have come out the back windows if she'd been upstairs when the fire started, wouldn't she? Some of the window panes were broke when I went in before. Before the whole lot blew. That'd be from her, right? That's how I'd have got out. Out the window and onto the back bedroom roof and then to the ground. It's not such a long way down. Not if you do it right.'

A wild hope, nothing more, but Po offered it and Jake clung to it. He stood up and moved forward a few steps, with one hand to a wall already hot to the touch.

He heard a whoosh, a great muffled rush of sound, and then the dojo roof came down and flames licked the sky. He looked for Po but the boy had disappeared. 'Po!'

He raced towards the back door of the building whose roof Po had commandeered. The door wasn't locked. How the hell would the kid get down? How the hell had he got up there in the first place?

'Po.' Roaring up the stairs but there was no sound of a boy coming down fast. Out onto the street, then, and into evacuation chaos. Sirens and blockades and everyone moving out, when all he wanted was to get in.

And then the boy stood in front of him. Hair singed and filthy. Blistered skin running diagonally across one of his arms. Burnt. Jake registered all these things as he scooped the boy up in his arms and held him close. Burnt while trying to find Jianne. 'You shouldn't have gone in there,' he said again, and held the boy tighter.

'You would have.'

'We need to get that arm of yours looked at.'

'No.' The boy held him tighter. 'We need to find her. She'll be here. Somewhere. She will.'

Fear and desolation. Adrenalin and pain.

As they scoured the crowd for a face they couldn't see, hope turned to ash and the ash was everywhere. He called Luke but Luke and Maddy were already scouring the crowd, searching for *them*. They hadn't found Ji.

Jake met up with Luke and Madeline on the corner nearest the place where dojo doors had once stood. No getting any closer to the building now. Not for anyone. Even the firefighters were keeping their distance now as they shot water high into the sky in a futile attempt to salvage something. Another muted whoosh sounded in Jake's ears as something else came crashing down inside the inferno.

'Po's arm,' he said hoarsely as the surreal orange glow from the fire burned up his eyes. 'It needs seeing to.'

'No,' said the boy and clung to him tighter. 'Find Jianne.'

Always the way, so many priorities piling in on a man at once but Jake was with the boy on this. Finding Jianne wasn't just a priority. It rated right up there with breathing. 'We'll go this way,' he muttered.

'Wait,' said Madeline, her eyes wide and worried but her composure not yet shattered. 'Po, how about you and I try the ambulance again and they can take a look at that arm while we're there, and we can make it our base? It's the first place Jianne will look for you. It's the first place everyone looks.' Madeline, who hadn't yet stripped down to core needs and instinct. Madeline who could still think.

'She's right,' said Luke, adding his not inconsiderable influence over the boy to the mix. 'You and Maddy at the ambulance. Me and Jake circling the block. We'll cover lots of ground that way.'

A new plan. A sane plan, with everyone's major needs met. And Luke went left and Jake turned right, scanning the sea of faces in front of him and putting one foot in front of the other. She'd be here somewhere. She had to be. He'd find her.

But he didn't.

He kept on walking, searching, hoping. As his livelihood and his home burned down behind him.

Just a building, love. He could say that when he found her. It's not important, it's just a building and there was no one in it.

So many different faces, curiosity and concern alike, and never the one he wanted most to see.

He stood there in the end. Just stood and let the crowd flow past him, too shattered to move. Maybe Zhi Fu had Jianne. Zhi Fu could have come and taken her and then set fire to the dojo for good measure. Maybe that was why Jake couldn't find her, why Po hadn't seen her. Better that than dead. She couldn't be dead.

Forward again then. One step and then another. Look, he told himself. *Look*.

And then he turned the street corner and he thought he caught a glimpse of a face more beloved than any other, just a glimpse, up ahead and then it was gone. But it gave him hope, such a wild desperate hope, and it gave his legs speed as he surged forward against the flow of the crowd. It felt like eternity before he saw her again, closer to him this time, coming towards him with the crowd.

Jianne.

Battered and filthy, as filthy as Po. Torn shirt and bleeding knees, but walking, and breathing and searching every face in the crowd, just as he'd been doing. She saw him and stopped and he felt the jolt of her recognition punch through him like a fist and following that fist came searing need wrapped in unspeakable relief.

She started towards him, her steps slow and unsteady. His weren't much better.

She'd been in that blaze but death had not taken her. So battered but not broken when she finally stood in front of him. 'The dojo's gone,' she said.

'I know.' He lifted his hand to her face and pushed a strand of singed hair out of her eyes. 'It doesn't matter.' He couldn't hold her—not the way he wanted to. 'Are you burnt?'

'I'm not sure,' she said raggedly. 'A lot of things hurt, but I don't think I'm burnt.'

'You went out the window,' he murmured. 'Po said you would.'

'I did.'

He put his hand to her cheek; that much he could touch without touching on hurt. He stepped in close and took a shuddering breath as the fear he'd held at bay surged up and threatened to overwhelm him. 'I thought I'd lost you.'

CHAPTER ELEVEN

Jacob looked haunted. As if he'd stood at the hell mouth and they'd dragged him inside. He stood there staring at Jianne and he was still inside, caught up somewhere in a reality she couldn't see. She touched him, touched his beloved face, touched her fingers to his lips and he drew a shuddering breath. Her warrior was trembling. Close to breaking.

'You haven't lost me,' she whispered. 'I'm right here. See?'

'I thought I'd failed you.' He closed his eyes. 'Again.'

'No,' she said. 'I brought this madness here, not you. And I wish I'd never come.'

'Don't say that,' he said. 'Never say that.' And he opened his eyes and set his lips to hers in a kiss so sweet and reverent that she wept beneath the purity of it. Buildings could be rebuilt. Businesses re-established. And love could heal as well as destroy.

She'd had a plan. Before the fire. Before the world had gone up in flames. A plan to tell this man who'd taken her in and risked everything for her—and lost everything on account of her—exactly what he meant to her.

'Whatever you want…whatever you need to start over…there's money there to rebuild all this and you damn well better take it.'

But Jacob just shook his head and took her lips again and this time she wrapped her arms around his neck and surrendered completely to his possession.

'I love you,' she whispered when finally he buried his face in her neck and his arms tightened around her. 'I love you beyond measure. I always have and I always will. Just so you know.'

Zhi Fu found them at the hospital. The hospital the ambulance driver had taken Jianne to—not because she was critically injured, but because it was smart and, no matter how much Jianne protested that she was okay, neither Jacob nor the ambulance crew were taking any chances. She'd cut her hands coming out of the window and she'd grazed them again during her fall to the ground; her hands were a mess and other parts of her weren't much better.

'I'm okay,' she'd kept telling him. 'You can stop worrying about me. Worry about something else. Worry about Po.'

But Po was just fine. He'd been patched up already and Maddy and Luke had taken him home to Maddy's where Po would spend the night. Jake was slowly coming to terms with the notion that he didn't always have to take sole responsibility for everything and everyone. There were others he could lean on now if need be. He just had to get used to the idea of relinquishing control every now and then, that was all.

Nothing like a blazing inferno to remind a man how much control he *didn't* have over some things.

Nothing like watching Sun Zhi Fu walking towards them to remind a man of the things he could do, and would do, to protect the woman he loved.

He stilled. Waited. Went to that quiet place deep inside where a beast sat waiting, waiting to be unleashed. Jianne put her bandaged-hand to Jacob's forearm. Two bandage wrapped hands, a scorched throat, soot-scraped eyes and too many cuts and bruises to count. Jacob catalogued her injuries one by one as the other man approached and the beast drank down that information and looked upon the man as prey.

Jianne knew they were in trouble the minute Jacob stilled and she looked up to see Zhi Fu heading their way. Dangerous man with hard agate eyes. Stupid *stupid* man if he thought he could approach Jacob now and come away unscathed.

Zhi Fu's hard black gaze swept her from head to toe, missing nothing, and Jianne could have sworn that just for a moment she saw anguish in his eyes.

'I didn't do this,' he said, and he said it in English so that Jacob would understand. 'I am not responsible for this fire.'

'Then who is?' she said fiercely. 'This wasn't an accident.' She felt Jacob's tension. She'd made a similar statement to the police but they'd been non-committal. They'd know soon enough how the fire first started, they'd told her. And they would be in touch. 'Someone torched the dojo deliberately.'

'Not I.' Zhi Fu's gaze flickered to Jacob and well it should have. Jianne stepped between the two men, her back towards Jacob. Jacob was no threat to her. She could hardly say the same for Zhi Fu.

'Why should we believe you?' she said. 'Why s.
I believe you? After all the things you've done.'

'What have I ever done except show you what I can
give you?'

'You sent a killer after my husband.'

'To beat him, not kill him.'

'You asked me if I wanted him *dead*.'

'To frighten you into giving him up,' said Zhi Fu
bleakly. 'I don't kill. It's the one boundary I've never
crossed. It's the only boundary I haven't crossed.'

'I don't believe you,' said Jianne.

'I will say it again,' said Zhi Fu. 'I didn't set this
fire or pay someone to do it for me. It's not a risk I was
willing to take. I don't kill. And I certainly don't try and
kill *you*.'

'I don't know what you thought to achieve by coming
here,' she said with an increasing lack of calm. She'd
thought to protect Jacob from rage by stepping in to
confront Zhi Fu. She'd forgotten about her own anger,
and the number of years it had been building. 'It's too
late for trust, and you can't win my love.'

'I can try.'

'You can *stop* trying,' she said. 'That's all I want
from you. It's the *only* thing I want from you. *Can't you
understand that?*'

They stared at one another in silence. Then Zhi Fu
reached into his pocket and held out a business card to
Jacob. 'I had a private investigator watching the dojo,'
he said. 'He has pictures of your arsonist on camera and
he's willing to speak to the police. As am I.'

'You really think you've done nothing wrong?' said
Jacob.

'I courted a woman with the intention of taking her for my wife,' said Zhi Fu smoothly. 'That's not a crime.'

'You sent a man to kill me,' said Jacob.

'Prove it.'

'You're *stalking* me,' said Jianne.

'Some would call that looking out for you.'

'I can look out for myself!'

'Really?' Zhi Fu looked her up and down again and lifted a cynical brow. 'Pardon my surprise. I've no intention of going into detail about the way you played me, Jianne. Hot and cold and hot and cold, though I'm sure the police would be sympathetic to my plight. I came here to see how badly you'd been hurt and to assist in the capture of your arsonist. I do this because I have feelings for you. Whether you reciprocate them or not.'

'Zhi Fu…' Such a slippery, complicated man. Not a good man; of that Jianne had never been more certain, but a man who was nonetheless offering some degree of help. 'Thank you for your concern and for your assistance. As for my feelings for you, I'm afraid they haven't changed so I'm asking you again—for the benefit of us all—to restructure your life so that I am not a part of it. I don't wish you ill…' Alas, not strictly true. 'All right, I might wish you *some* degree of ill but mostly I just want you to get on with your life. And let me live mine.'

'With him,' said Zhi Fu.

'Yes,' said Jianne, shooting Jacob a searching glance, he'd been largely silent throughout this exchange. So quiet. So chillingly contained. 'With him, if he'll have me.'

Jacob looked down at her then and hot and primal possession flared in his eyes. 'I'll have you,' he said quietly, and then turned his attention back to Zhi Fu.

'You need to leave,' said Jacob, and the deadly intent in his eyes turned Jianne's spine to ice. 'Go back to Shanghai. Leave my wife alone.'

'And if I don't?' said Zhi Fu.

'Then you and I have a problem,' said Jacob. 'Because I won't let Jianne live the way she's been living. In fear of you. Of what you'll try next. Of how you'll hurt and manipulate the people she loves. You talked of boundaries and the knowing of them. Happens I know mine as well and right or wrong they're a little more fluid than yours. You need to walk away. Now. Before you wind up in prison or you die.'

Zhi Fu and Jacob stared at one another for a very long time.

And then, without even looking at Jianne, Sun Zhi Fu took his leave.

Jianne and Jacob walked from the hospital a few minutes later. Jacob shoved his hands in his pockets and looked up at the sky. Jianne looked at Jacob and tried not to think too hard on all that had happened tonight. On all the things that Jacob had lost. She stood and she bled for him, just a little, and she rejoiced in him, this beautiful fire-forged man with not a possession in the world but for what was inside him. Honour and protectiveness: a warrior's way, and a heart that guided him true.

'So...' he said, with the hint of a tired smile. 'What now? Where to?'

'I don't know.'

'Your aunt and uncle will probably want to see you. See for themselves that you're all right.'

'I know.' But she didn't want to be cosseted by her family right now. 'I'll call them and tell them I'll see them soon but not tonight. Maybe tomorrow.'

'You want to go to Madeline and Luke's? See Po?'

'Yes.' Po the needy who'd burned in search of her. Po, who walked in his sensei's footsteps and had the makings of a man who could change the world. 'Will he blush if I kiss him, do you think?' she asked lightly. 'I think I embarrass him.'

'He likes it,' said Jacob. 'It's good for him. Embarrass him as much as you want.' Jacob shot her a smile then that would have stolen her heart had it not already been irrevocably his. 'We could find ourselves a hotel room for the night after that.'

'We could,' she agreed. 'Somewhere with an enormous bathtub and a view that runs for ever, and we could lie there in the water and I could try not to get these hands wet, and you could help me wash my hair. I don't know if you've noticed, but I'm all for *not* being covered in soot and smelling of fire smoke.'

'I could help you there,' he said gruffly. 'We could shower first and then soak in the bath and stare at the view and I could mention—in case you hadn't noticed—how deeply in love I am with my wife.'

'You could,' she said gravely. 'Although the bandages would likely get wet after that.'

'I could always distract you by asking you for your thoughts on what the future might hold for us.' Jacob looked to the stars again. 'The dojo's gone but so are the limitations that went with it. Clean slate, Ji. A chance to build a life together. Whatever we want, however we want it.'

'There could be a rooftop garden,' she murmured. On top of the dojo.'

'Dojo?' he queried with a swift searching glance in her direction.

'I know what teaching brings to you, sensei,' she said gently. 'I know what you are. How you're made. And what you bring to others. Do you *not* want to rebuild the dojo?'

He didn't say anything for quite some time after that.

'There could be underground parking,' he said finally. 'For cars.'

'Another floor in between the training hall and the upstairs bedroom,' she said. 'For the children.'

'Children?'

'Mm'm.' She countered another searching glance with a quietly challenging look of her own. 'Ours. Strays. Nieces and nephews who've come to Singapore to learn karate. I'm in if you are.'

'I'm in,' he murmured. 'All the way in.' And after a pause, 'I liked what you did with the kitchen.'

'Then we'll do it again,' she said with the beginnings of a grin. 'There can be tongs.'

'And bowls that break.'

'They won't break.'

'I love you,' he said.

'I know.' As she stepped in close and Jacob wrapped his arms around her. 'I love you too. With all of my heart.'

EPILOGUE

Singapore, two years later...

MORNING came softly to some. It crept up on them one slow and languid stretch at a time. Jianne's mornings often started that way, much to Jacob's amusement and lazy satisfaction. He loved the smile that stole over Jianne's lips when she sensed that he was awake and watching her. He loved the way her eyes would open and fix on him, and there'd be a smile in them too, along with a promise.

Two years married—remarried—and it only got better. Zhi Fu had stopped his pursuit of Jianne and returned to Shangahi. According to Jianne's mother, Zhi Fu had recently taken a wife. Jake and Jianne hadn't been invited to the wedding.

Po had disappeared in the days following the burning of the dojo. Disappeared and then reappeared at a Singapore police station three days later, bruised and beaten, with a three-year-old girl and a six-year-old boy in tow. His half-brother and sister—with their mother dead, as Po's mother was dead, and a vengeful arsonist for a father. The justice system had taken care of Po's father. Po's half-siblings had been taken in by their maternal grandmother. Po's father had been the boy's only living relative, so Jake and Jianne—with the aid of the best lawyers money could buy—had won the right to care for Po until the boy reached his majority. Beyond then, too, for Po was theirs now—now and for ever—a Bennett of the heart and to hell with blood.

Out of the ashes of misfortune more than one phoenix had risen.

A boy so wise and gifted and hungry to make a difference that Jake could barely wait to see what Po would become.

A dojo had been rebuilt in the exact place where only ashes had remained. A dojo and a home—complete with underground parking, rooftop garden, a children's wing, office space for Jianne, and ample guest accommodation for both family and students.

And a marriage had flourished.

Jianne Xang-Bennett loved her husband, loved him well and often, and Jake revelled in it, fed on it, and counted himself the most fortunate man in the world because of it. Whether fortune favoured the brave or whether every man was the architect of his own fortune—he didn't care. Jake had his family, he had everything he'd ever wanted and he was never letting go.

Jacob slid from his bed without waking Jianne, and padded silently into the adjoining room and over to where someone *was* awake. A tiny baby girl with rosebud lips, silky black hair, and eyes so dark and beautiful that he melted every time she looked his way. She didn't have a name—not yet. He and Jianne were running a little late in that regard.

From the moment she'd slid out of her mother, red-faced and roaring with fury, she'd captured his heart.

A midwife had handed the screaming bundle to him, and she'd stopped on a hiccup, and stared at him with dark, slightly unfocused eyes. Her tiny fern-like fist had unfurled and he'd touched it in wonder, marvelling at her perfection. And she'd closed her impossibly tiny hand around his finger, and gripped hard, and with that one gesture she had captured his soul for ever.

'Like her father,' Jianne had said with a smile. 'What she has, she holds.'

'Like her mother,' he'd responded. 'Impossibly beautiful.'

His brother Luke had taken one look at Jake holding his baby daughter and said, 'Man, she is so cute.' And then the baby had grabbed Luke's hair in an imperious grip, and he'd muttered, 'And we are so screwed.'

'Trouble,' said Po, when he first held Jake's daughter, but that didn't stop the boy from wanting to carry trouble with him wherever he went. Trouble had a willing slave and his name was Po.

Jake simply thought of her as *beloved*.

'You're going to meet your aunts and uncles today,' Jake told the tiny girl as he lifted her from her crib and settled her against his chest. 'And your cousins. They're here for your christening.' Hence the slight urgency surrounding the baby's name. 'Your aunt Hallie will probably try and scare you with talk of wide brimmed hats and pinafore dresses that end at your ankles but don't you take any notice of her. The Bennett brothers have moved on. I'm sure if you carry a parasol and keep your knees covered, everything will be just fine.'

The poppet nuzzled his chest and thumped him with a tiny fist. Jake's besotted smile turned wry. 'I'm taking that as a *"yes, Daddy"*.'

Jake offered up a finger and his daughter grasped it with tiny fingers. 'And don't you give your cousins any grief, either. They may be wild, but they'll be there for you when you need them, until the end of time. It's how Bennetts are made. Never forget that.'

The tiny baby brought her fist to her mouth, with Jake's finger still locked firmly in her grasp.

'She's hungry,' said a voice from behind him, and then Jianne was sliding her arm around his waist and setting gentle fingers to her daughter's head.

'I know.' Jake tried to extricate his finger but his baby held firm. 'She won't let go.'

'Smart girl,' said Jianne. 'I wouldn't either.'

'She's so fragile,' murmured Jake. Such a delicate little thing to hold him in such thrall.

'She's stronger than she looks.' Jianne rested her cheek against his shoulder. 'She has her father's heart. A heart from which others take strength. A tiger's heart.'

'Is that a warning?' asked Jake.

'It probably should be,' murmured Jianne. 'But I prefer to think of it as a blessing. It's also all your fault, by the way. And I've thought of a name. Our daughter will need a strong name.'

'You're not calling her Tiger,' said Jake.

Jianne smiled serenely. 'I thought Willow. One who bends but never breaks, no matter how wild the storm. In Chinese it would be Lian. Lian-li if you like, although the second name is more traditionally a boy's name or a surname. It means strength.'

'Pretty,' said Jake. And to the baby, 'What do you think, Li-li? Are you strong enough for such a name?'

'Of course she is,' said Jianne with a swift kiss for his cheek and then a more lingering greeting for his mouth. 'She's a Bennett.'

Coming Next Month

Harlequin Presents

#2981 FLORA'S B...
Lynne Graham
Secretly Pregnant...Conveniently...

from ... **...esents®**. Available March 29, 2011.

#2982 THE RETURN OF THE RENE...
Carole Mortimer
The Scandalous St. Claires

#2983 NOT FOR SALE
Sandra Marton

#2984 BEAUTY AND THE GREEK
Kim Lawrence

#2985 AN ACCIDENTAL BIRTHRIGHT
Maisey Yates

#2986 THE DEVIL'S HEART
Lynn Raye Harris

Coming Next Month

from **Harlequin Presents® EXTRA**. Available April 12, 2011.

#145 PICTURE OF INNOCENCE
Jacqueline Baird
Italian Temptation!

#146 THE PROUD WIFE
Kate Walker
Italian Temptation!

#147 SURF, SEA AND A SEXY STRANGER
Heidi Rice
One Hot Fling

#148 WALK ON THE WILD SIDE
Natalie Anderson
One Hot Fling

REQUEST YO...
FREE BOO...

HARLEQUIN *Presents*

PASSION GUARANTEED SEDUCTION

2 FREE NOVELS...!
2 FREE GI...

YES! Please send m... 2 FREE Harlequin Presents® novels and my 2 FREE gifts (gifts are worth about $10). After receiving them, if I don't wish to receive any more books, I can return the shipping statement marked "cancel." If I don't cancel, I will receive 6 brand-new novels every month and be billed just $4.05 per book in the U.S. or $4.74 per book in Canada. That's a saving of at least 15% off the cover price! It's quite a bargain! Shipping and handling is just 50¢ per book.* I understand that accepting the 2 free books and gifts places me under no obligation to buy anything. I can always return a shipment and cancel at any time. Even if I never buy another book, the two free books and gifts are mine to keep forever.

106/306 HDN E5M4

Name _____ (PLEASE PRINT)

Address _____ Apt. #

City _____ State/Prov. _____ Zip/Postal Code

Signature (if under 18, a parent or guardian must sign)

Mail to the Harlequin Reader Service:
IN U.S.A.: P.O. Box 1867, Buffalo, NY 14240-1867
IN CANADA: P.O. Box 609, Fort Erie, Ontario L2A 5X3

Not valid for current subscribers to Harlequin Presents books.

Are you a current subscriber to Harlequin Presents books and want to receive the larger-print edition? Call 1-800-873-8635 today!

* Terms and prices subject to change without notice. Prices do not include applicable taxes. N.Y. residents add applicable sales tax. Canadian residents will be charged applicable provincial taxes and GST. Offer not valid in Quebec. This offer is limited to one order per household. All orders subject to approval. Credit or debit balances in a customer's account(s) may be offset by any other outstanding balance owed by or to the customer. Please allow 4 to 6 weeks for delivery. Offer available while quantities last.

Your Privacy: Harlequin Books is committed to protecting your privacy. Our Privacy Policy is available online at www.eHarlequin.com or upon request from the Reader Service. From time to time we make our lists of customers available to reputable third parties who may have a product or service of interest to you. If you would prefer we not share your name and address, please check here. ☐

Help us get it right—We strive for accurate, respectful and relevant communications. To clarify or modify your communication preferences, visit us at www.ReaderService.com/consumerchoice.

HP10R

You were right to turn my marri... offer down," Aristedes said.

And Selene found her voice at last, found the words that would not betray the blow he'd dealt her. "Thanks for letting me know. You didn't have to come all the way here, though. You could have just let it go. I left yesterday with the understanding that this case is closed."

Before the hot needles behind her eyes could dissolve into an unforgivable display of stupidity and weakness, she began to close the door.

The door stopped against an immovable object. His flat palm.

"I can't accept that." His voice was low, leashed.

What did her tormentor mean now? Was he ending one game only to start another?

She raised eyes as bruised as her self-respect to his, found nothing there but solemnity and determination.

Before she could voice her confusion, he elaborated. "I never let anything go unless I'm certain it's unworkable. I realize I made you an unworkable offer, and that's why I'm withdrawing it. I'm here to offer something else. A workability study."

She leaned against the door, thankful for its support and partial shield. "Your son and I are not a business venture you can test for feasibility."

His gaze grew deeper, made her feel as if he was trying to delve into her mind, take control of it. "It's actually the were emitting ... you nor I have any reaso... ...or both you and Ale... only truth. It might be ... hear from me again ... forget I exist. But then again, mayb... not. I'm only a...ing for the chance for both of us to find out for certain. You believe I'm unworkable in any personal relationship. I've lived my life based on that belief about myself. I never really had reason to question it. But I have one now. In fact, I have two."

Find out what happens in
THE SARANTOS SECRET BABY by Olivia Gates,
available April 2011, only from Harlequin Desire.

Harlequin® Blaze™

red-hot reads

Sunny, sensual Hawaiian spring break…again!

Three best girlfriends are recapturing an amazing spring-break vacation they had a decade ago.

First on the beach is former attorney and all-around good girl Mia Butterfield. Meeting up with her boyfriend of old is a bust, so she's shocked when her hero turns out to be someone she'd never have expected…

Find out who it is in
SECOND TIME LUCKY
by acclaimed author
Debbi Rawlins

Available from Harlequin Blaze® April 2011

Part of the sensual miniseries,
Spring Break

Part 2: Delicious Do-Over (May)

Harlequin®

A *Romance* FOR EVERY MOOD™

www.eHarlequin.com

HB79607